BRENDA BROSTER

authorHOUSE®

AuthorHouse™ UK
1663 Liberty Drive
Bloomington, IN 47403 USA
www.authorhouse.co.uk
Phone: 0800.197.4150

Published by AuthorHouse 08/19/2016

ISBN: 978-1-5246-6143-4 (sc)
ISBN: 978-1-5246-6142-7 (e)

Print information available on the last page.

This book is printed on acid-free paper.

For all those who devote their lives to
the conservation and preservation
of this planet and those who inhabit it.

This is a work of fiction. Any
similarity or resemblance
To actual persons, living or
dead, is coincidental.
The characters within this book are the
creations of the author's imagination.

"Until we extend our circle of compassion to all living things, humanity will not find peace."

Albert Schweitzer
The Philosophy of Civilization

CHAPTER 1

Rambut Sutera, of the Orang-Asli tribe, was in the forest gathering fresh herbs after the rain. In the monsoon season the rains were heavy. The ground under foot was slippery, the undergrowth was sodden, and the bushes and trees dripped incessantly. Over and above the dripping leaves, the singing cicadas and various other forest noises, scuffling, rustling, animal noises, his sharp ears picked up muffled sounds. He stopped and strained his ears; the sounds were coming from some way off. Carefully, he followed the sounds. As he drew closer, they became clearer, a terrible crying, howling noise – a creature in trouble.

Treading softly along the hidden trail, he almost fell into the old bear pit before he saw it. A bear was trapped down there, a female bear, deeply distressed. The pit was half full of water, the ground around it slippery and treacherous. The exhausted, sodden creature was thrashing about at the bottom of the pit, gnawing at the sides, crying, desperately trying to get a hold with her long strong claws and climb out. It looked as if she had been there for a couple of days. The man spoke quietly to the bear and the sound of his voice calmed her. He told her he would get help, and went off at a trot to fetch other members of his tribe.

In only a little time Rambut Sutera returned with half a dozen men. They brought with them long lianas, strong enough to support the weight of the bear, and atap mats which would protect the bear's flesh from being cut by the lianas as they lifted her. The bear, seeing they were trying to help her, stopped thrashing about, and allowed them to lower the lianas and atap mats into the pit. Skillfully they drew them around her and, when ready, all hauling together, they pulled her slowly upwards, lifting her, inch by painful inch, out of the pit. Eventually on solid ground, they unwound the ropes and matting from the bear, and she was free. But she did not run off, as they expected. She padded backwards and forwards, sniffing the ground, sniffing the air. She was desperate, crying large watery tears, calling as she searched. The Orang-Asli watched her in dismay. Where were her cubs? She was searching for them. Something was wrong. They must tell the headman about this - the bear was inconsolable.

Deep in the forest, Matahari and Cahaya Bulan were quietly rejoicing at the birth of their new baby son. He was perfect in every way; his little toenails were still pink, as was the tip of his trunk, and the edges of his ears were pink too, but they would get darker as he got older, and he would grow into a fine, strong elephant like his father. His skin was smooth and soft, and his little head was topped with soft, tufty black hair. Cahaya Bulan caressed him gently with her trunk, pulling him closer to her. This baby was very precious. Eventually, he would succeed Matahari as undisputed King of the Forest. He would inherit all the responsibility which went with that role. But, for the time being, until he grew up, Cahaya Bulan would nurture and protect him as much as she could. Here, deep in the forest, surrounded by his tribe, he was safe.

Tunku, as was his custom in the heat of the afternoon, was resting high up in the leafy forest canopy. It was cool up here. He snored gently. Since the great battle with the evil palm oil baron's men, life in the forest had been reasonably tranquil. There was the occasional hunt, of course. Carnivores must have meat; besides, the hunts disposed of the weak and infirm. Apart from that, Tunku had no complaints; it was a long time since any aspiring young male orang utan had challenged his undisputed authority as leader of his tribe, King of the Canopies.

Life was good, and he was dozing. He was woken by Number One Son, who was to have his naming day in a week's time. That would be a big day, and there would be feasting in the forest. Number One Son would one day inherit Tunku's own responsibilities: to look after his tribe and, indeed, the well-being of the forest as a whole. This responsibility Tunku shared with Matahari, the King of the Elephants. Between them, they maintained peace and ensured that all the creatures lived more or less in harmony. Number One Son would, of course, have to fight off hot-headed aspiring young contenders, just as Tunku, his father, had done before him. But Tunku had taught his son well and had no doubt that Number One Son would succeed him.

Tunku stretched contentedly, his long seemingly endless arms reaching up through the branches. Flexing his long, slim fingers, he opened his mouth in a huge yawn revealing big, yellow teeth, and gently shook himself, his cheek flaps and silken red coat swaying with the motion.

Hitam Malam, the big moon bear, was padding swiftly along the forest trail. He needed to find Tunku. Hitam Malam was deeply distressed and disturbed; his big head rolled from side to side. Number One Son, ever alert and on the look-out for anything untoward, spotted Hitam Malam, far below on the trail; he had not seen him for some time. He bound down the tree trunk. Landing with a somersault in front of Hitam Malam, Number One Son greeted him with pleasure. Hitam Malam scarcely had time to return Number One Son's greeting. He told him that he was looking for Tunku, and it was urgent. He would say no more. Hitam Malam could be grumpy, Number One Son knew, but he was always courteous. Number One Son was surprised at his abruptness.

Number One Son led Hitam Malam to Tunku's refuge. Climbing up into the canopy, he told Tunku that Hitam Malam was waiting down below in the forest and wanted to have a word with him. As Tunku had not seen Hitam

Malam since the great fight, he wondered what was amiss. The big bear would not come to him unless he had very good reason. Generally, Hitam Malam liked his own company, mixing rarely with the other creatures. Slowly, he only ever moved quickly if it was essential, Tunku climbed down to the ground below.

Hitam Malam was pacing back and forth impatiently. (Bears are not known for their patience, and Hitam Malan was no exception). He and Tunku had a long talk, and then Hitam Malam set off at a lope. Number One Son could see him following one of the trails to the mangrove swamp. Deep in thought, Tunku climbed back up the tree to his platform where Number One Son was waiting. He sat in silence while Number One Son waited patiently. Eventually, Tunku stirred.

"There is trouble in the forest again," he said. "I think you must tell Matahari." Number One Son was a little afraid of Matahari, 'Lord of the Jungle'. He was the biggest elephant Number One Son had ever seen, very black, with great long tusks.

Tunku was getting old. Badly wounded in the great battle, he had never really recovered his strength and vitality. Now, he frequently used Number One Son as a messenger. It was good for him to learn how to run the forest, and would stand him in good stead when the time came for him to take over Tunku's role as Keeper of the Canopies. There was much to learn.

Number One Son set off to find Matahari, who was deep in the damp forest with his new family. Meanwhile, Tunku thought that he had better go and see his wife, Puteri, and their baby son, Number Two, who was growing up fast. There was trouble ahead.

Puteri and Number Two Son were chomping happily on Mangosteens when Tunku arrived. She was pleased to see him. Tunku joined her in the feast and, when they were sated, he told her Hitam Malam's news. Puteri was worried. *'Oh no!. The poor bears.'* she thought. Pulling Number Two Son closer to her, she hugged him tightly.

"I have sent Number One Son to tell Matahari. I must go to the glade and meet him there." Tunku told her.

"Is that wise? You are not as young as you were." Puteri always worried about Tunku. She knew how much he had suffered after the big battle, and there was no doubt he was slowing down.

"Yes, I must go," Tunku said decisively. "I shall set off today."

"Be careful," warned Puteri, giving him a hug and kissing him – a big smacking kiss – on the lips. "Number Two Son and I will be here, waiting for you."

The children had been back at school for a full term after the summer holidays and had been very busy since the great fight. They had been feted by the Prime Minister, the media and the public. In a way, they were famous, and all because of the big fight. It was most bewildering. After all, they had only tried to save the forest. Well, they had succeeded, but a lot of people were making a big fuss about it. Their pictures had been in the papers, in magazines, lots of photographs which Bert, the photographer, had taken. They had been on television. Even their parents had been interviewed. And all that on top of going to school and doing their homework every day. They were still receiving e.mails on a daily basis from all over the world. Everything was so exciting, it had been hard settling down to school routine again. But Miss Thompson, their headmistress, had been very helpful.

In fact, she was delighted, because parents were now queuing up to send their children to her school. The parents were apparently impressed by the intelligence, initiative and ingenuity of the children she taught (as depicted by the five Doughty Warriors, as they had been dubbed by Shirley Pooper).

Indeed, Miss Thompson had a word with Professor Profundo, and it was agreed that Botany, Ecology, and Pharmacognosis should forthwith be incorporated in the school curriculum. Professor Profundo had put forward Yusof's name as an excellent potential teacher, and it had been agreed that Yusof would teach at the school three mornings a week. This pleased Yusof because it made him a little extra money, which he immediately recirculated into his charity for the protection of the forest and its creatures, it gave him a small pension, which would be very useful in the future, and, above all, meant he could spread the word about the importance of saving the forest and its creatures. This was his passion. Ibrahim and Faradilla were very proud of their father.

"What are we to do this holiday?" asked Vinod.

"I shall go to the forest with Bapa, I think," said Ibrahim, thoughtful as ever. "He needs a lot of help building the rescue centre. He wants to make it as smart as possible, so people can come and learn about the animals." Ibrahim, as ever, was thoughtful.

"But our last holiday was soooo... exciting," said Faradilla with feeling.

"I, for one, shall enjoy helping Yusof," added Joseph. "But we have so many emails coming in asking for help, and there is a lot of stuff coming in on Twitter too. I'm sure we can do something else, help someone. But with so many emails, and so many people wanting help, I do wonder what we can possibly do." Joseph was genuinely worried by the burden of responsibility sitting heavily on his shoulders.

"Well, let's think about it" said Xin-Hui. "Let's make a list of the e.mails, and see which ones we think we can do something about."

Joseph looked at her. *'Why is Xin-Hui always so practical?'* he wondered. "O.K." They all sat down and started to work.

Joseph and Ibrahim, the two eldest, had received most emails. Vinod and Xin-Hui had received some, and Faradilla was too young, but she was growing up fast.

"There's this one about the turtles" "Ooooh! I like turtles."

"And this one about the coral reefs, and the one about the sharks."

"A lot of them are weird. Look at this one asking us to stop governments owning land. I think it's from a nutter."

"And then the one asking us to stop oil rigs. Or what about that one which wanted us to go to Australia and protect the cockatoos?" "Ooh, I should like to do that."

"Yes, but it is not practical. We are only children." Xin-Hui, as usual, was right.

"We should each make a short-list of the things we think we are most likely to be able to do. And then we'll get together with our shortlists, and decide if there is one we can do something about. We are only children." Joseph repeated Xin-Hui's sentiment. After all, the great fight had been accidental really. They had fallen into it by chance. It was not as if they had planned to get involved from the outset. And all these emails were rather overwhelming.

"I wonder what Toby's doing. Do you think he will come out for the holiday?"

"I know he wants to, but it depends on the Professor." Ibrahim looked rueful. He really hoped Toby would be able to join them.

"We will think about our emails. We shall have a great holiday. Do not worry." Vinod said, grinning cheekily. Vinod was determined to support some cause or other. He did not particularly mind which one, but he wanted the activity, the excitement. The great fight with the evil palm oil baron's men had been so exciting. His eyes widened as he thought of it. *'So exciting!'*

He jumped up, yelling "Race you to the pool."

Laughing, they raced to the pool, Faradilla, as usual, bringing up the rear. Diving in, they splashed and swam like fishes, as if they did not have a care in the world.

CHAPTER 2

Frantically, Hitam Malam was searching for members of his family. He had to know. Everyone needed to be accounted for. As he padded along, his brain was racing. ' *Two cubs known about. How many more? Who has taken them? Where have they gone?'* Orkid, their mother, was inconsolable. Hitam Malam knew that if they were to be found, the whole forest would have to be geared into action. And they must move fast, very fast. Once the cubs were out of the forest, there would be little chance of ever finding them.' He quickened his pace, praying to the Great God of the Bears *'Please do not let there be any more.'*

Ibrahim was deep in the forest with his father, Yusof, gathering herbs and bark for Yusof's research, and for medicines. Yusof treated all the creatures in his care with herbal medicines he prepared himself, and they worked extraordinarily well. Swinging through the canopy above, Number One Son saw them far below. He had played with Ibrahim for many years and they were old friends. He descended to greet them. Ibrahim was thrilled to see Number One Son again. He had not seen any of Tunku's family for a long time. Number One Son told him that there was a problem, something to do with Hitam Malam, and that he was on his way to tell Matahari that Tunku needed a conference. Ibrahim then conveyed this message to Yusof.

"Tell Tunku we shall do whatever we can to help" said Yusof.

Number One Son invited Ibrahim, Yusof, Professor Profundo, and all the other children to his naming day in a week's time. This invitation was an enormous privilege. Humans, apart from the Orang Asli, had NEVER previously attended such ceremonies. Yusof and Ibrahim were delighted to accept the invitation, and promised to tell the others. *'Little Number One Son is growing up fast. He is no longer little.'* thought Yusof as he watched Number One Son, sleek and glossy, muscles rippling, hurrying on his way. Tunku had told him there was no time to waste.

"If Tunku needs a conference, it must be big trouble, Bapa" said Ibrahim.

"Yes, My Son" agreed Yusof. Like Ibrahim, he was concerned. *'What could the problem possibly be?'* The evil palm oil baron was banished, so could no longer harm them. He wondered whether perhaps he should talk to the Headman of the Orang Asli. *'Yes'* he realized, *'that is what I must do.'*

Hitam Malam was calling. His cousins were certainly here. Clearly agitated, Hantu, his favourite cousin, came racing towards him with the news that they had lost three cubs. He told Hitam Malam they had lost three cubs, and that he suspected more had been taken.

Hitam Malam's worst fears were confirmed. This was terrible. Quickly, he instructed Hantu to round up the tribe, find out exactly how many cubs had been taken, and when. Then, without further ado, he headed off to the glade by the mangrove swamp. If Tunku had found Matahari, that is where they would meet. But it would take time to get there.

Matahari and Cahaya Bulan had agreed to name their small son Guruh. It was a fitting name for the future King of the Jungle. They were introducing him, for the first time, to the river. Initially he was frightened, but he quickly followed his mother into the water where she taught him to suck up as much water as he could with his trunk and then spurt it out. He thought that was great fun and was soon rolling and frolicking delightedly in the water with his parents. That is where Number One Son found them. Standing on the river bank, he grinned as he watched the elephant family playing together. He would have joined them but he did not much like water. Instead, he called to Matahari who lumbered slowly, trunk swinging, towards him. Matahari was surprised to see Number One Son and realized that it must be a serious matter to have brought him here.

Number One Son told Matahari that Tunku wished to meet him urgently on a very grave matter. He did not know what it was, except that it was something grave. Understanding that Tunku would not send for him unnecessarily, Matahari took his leave of Cahaya Bulan and Guruh and set off for the glade. Number One Son, wasting no more time, made his way back to Tunku as fast as he could.

Yusof set off to find the headman of the Orang Asli, Ibrahim trotting along behind him. There was no way Ibrahim was going to be left out of this. The heavy rains had soaked the ground to such an extent that water lay on top of it, unable to drain away. The earth below had turned to slippery mud, which made the going difficult. They slipped and slithered along the forest trails, making for the Orang Asli village, deep in the forest, and known to only a very few people. Brushing away the heavy undergrowth as they went, and dripped on by the trees, Yusof and Ibrahim were soon soaked through. In good weather, the walk to the village would take them only hours, but this time it would take all day. They realized they would have to stay overnight in the village. Ibrahim had not stayed in the Orang-Asli village before. It was a privilege and an honour to be allowed to do so. In fact, Yusof was the only outsider, as far as Ibrahim was aware, who had EVER been allowed to stay there.

By time they arrived at the village, Yusof and Ibrahim were very tired. Dusk had fallen and buffalo were grazing contentedly on the outskirts of the village. Ibrahim saw that the atap houses were all built on stilts. *'Sensible in this weather,'* he thought. Each long house had an anjung around it but the important thing was that they were dry and smoke was coming from a sort of chimney in one of the houses, the biggest one. Ibrahim was hungry and could smell something delicious cooking. *'Food! Hot food!'* Men, women, children, dogs, cockerels, chickens, and even goats, were milling about everywhere. Some of the cockerels, the white ones, contained in wicker baskets on the ground had their feathers dyed fuchsia pink. *'Very strange.'* Ibrahim knew the men of the village prized their fighting cocks very highly, and kept them as pets. The village was quiet, every villager seemed to have a purpose, and they were all cheerful. The headman, who was old and grizzled but still very strong, was sitting, cross-legged on the anjung. He spotted Yusof emerging from the forest, and, standing up, coming forward to the edge of the anjung to greet him, followed by a pack of dogs.

"Welcome, my Friend" he called. "What brings you to my village? Come, come and eat with us."

Yusof waved a greeting at the old man. They climbed the steps -a ladder really- fashioned out of bamboo poles, up to the anjung. They sat down together, cross-legged, facing each other. Ibrahim sat quietly, a little apart. They talked for a long time of many things, and they ate, and they talked again, until Yusof said casually "Something is afoot in the forest, old man. We met Number One Son who was delivering a message to Matahari saying that Tunku needed to see him urgently."

"Yes, something is amiss, but I do not know what. My people found a female bear trapped in a pit. There were no cubs and there should have been. If Tunku has called for Matahari they will meet in the glade. Perhaps I should go there."

"Can I come too?" Ibrahim chipped in. "I have been to the glade before." he reminded the old man.

The old man looked at Ibrahim but said nothing. He thought for a while, chewing on a betel leaf.

Finally, "We must sleep now," the head man finally said to Yusof." We shall set off in the morning and I shall take Ibrahim with me."

Yusof was pleased for Ibrahim. He knew that, more than anything, Ibrahim wanted to see Matahari and Tunku again, and the headman would teach him the ways of the forest.

They slept with the single men of the village in the longhouse, in little compartments like cubicles in a dormitory. As soon as dawn crept in, they rose and the headman and Ibrahim set off for the glade while Yusof made his way back to the kampong. Ibrahim liked this time of day best of all, the air was clear and it was still cool, not yet humid and sticky. And the rain had held off overnight which made the going easier. The headman knew the forest trails as well as any forest creature and they made good headway. Ibrahim loved the sounds of the birds, the monkeys calling, and the ever present cicadas calling their love songs. As they progressed, however silently, he was aware that monkeys were following them up in the trees. *'They are so curious,'* he thought. *'They never miss anything.'*

The Headman and Ibrahim eventually arrived in the glade at dusk. *'It looks very different now, so much bigger!'* thought Ibrahim. The last - and only - time he had been to the glade it had been full from one end to the other with animals of every kind. That had been an exciting night, never to be forgotten. Now it was empty, and still. He and the headman climbed into a tree and settled down to wait for Tunku and Matahari. The last time Ibrahim had been here the whole glade had been lit by fireflies but this time only a few were darting about, tiny pinpricks of light in the gloom. Ibrahim reached out and tried to catch one in his hand but it evaded him.

"Ssshhh!"

The headman had heard something. Ibrahim froze, still as a rock in the tree. He felt the earth tremble and tremble again. After waiting with bated breath for what seemed like an age, an enormous black shadow emerged from the other side of the glade. Ibrahim could scarcely see but he caught a gleam of white tusk in the moonlight. *'Hurrah! It's Matahari.'* he thought. The great black elephant, King of the Forest, moved slowly and silently forward until he was in the middle of the glade. There he stood, blowing softly down his trunk.

Instructing Ibrahim to stay where he was, the Headman climbed down from the tree, and made his way over to Matahari. Matahari snorted. He was pleased to see the old man. Then there was a rustling of leaves and Tunku dropped down beside them, another great shadow in the dark. Ibrahim was desperate to get out of the tree and join them but he had promised his father he would do as he was told and he had promised the Headman he would stay where he was. It was so dark, he could not see their faces. All he could see, if he really strained his eyes, were the approximate outlines of Matahari, the Headman, and Tunku. But then, just as he thought his eyes were becoming accustomed to the gloom,there was Tunku, standing directly below him.

"Hello, my old friend, come and join us."

Without hesitation, Ibrahim leaped out of the tree straight into Tunku's arms. Tunku chuckled. He and this small boy went back a long way. Ibrahim gave Tunku the biggest hug he could. They walked together to the centre of the glade where Matahari and the Headman were waiting. Matahari greeted Ibrahim with pleasure. He could not count the number of times he had borne this child on his back. Ibrahim was as much a child of the forest as any of the creatures and they all knew him well. Reaching out with his trunk, Matahari lifted Ibrahim on to his knee, from where Ibrahim was able to scramble up on to his back.

'Happiness!' The Headman smiled. He knew Ibrahim's affinity with the animals was exceptional. He explained to Ibrahim that they were waiting for Hitam Malam. They waited for several hours. The Headman and Tunku squatted down beside Matahari while Ibrahim dozed on the great elephant's back.

Hitam Malam came pounding into the glade. He was exhausted, and very distressed. Nine cubs in total had been taken. Two of the mothers had been killed, their paws hacked off, and their gall bladders cut out. Another had been enticed into a bear pit. Once she was in there, her cubs had been defenceless against four large men who had taken them away. The Orang Asli had rescued her. Hitam Malam thanked the Headman. Another bear, Keyakinan, had been netted and while she was helpless her cubs had also been taken. To escape, she had chewed desperately through the netting, assisted by a troop of monkeys who all had sharp teeth. She too had mentioned four large men. She had searched and searched but she could not find her cubs. Hitam Malam wept - he was acquainted with all these bears.

"We are so few. We cannot afford to lose our cubs. And, worse still, what is to become of them? I have heard terrible stories."

Matahari, Tunku and the Headman were grave. They had all heard the terrible stories. "The cubs have to be found. And before they leave the forest," said Hitam Malam, distraught.

They discussed the matter for a long time. When the conference in the glade came to an end, it was another new dawn. Ibrahim who had slept most of the night on Matahari's back climbed down and the Headman led him through the dark forest, back to his kampong. Ibrahim was exhausted so his mother, Aishah, sent him straight to bed. The mists were still rising on the marshes. Deep in conversation, the Headman walked off with Yusof.

Ibrahim slept for a long time. When he eventually awoke, he was totally refreshed.

"I have to see the others," he told his sister, Faradilla, "as soon as possible. I have our summer holiday task. I now know what we have to do." He was absolutely positive.

'What is it? What is it?" she cried.

"No. You must wait until the others get here."

Faradilla had great difficulty containing her patience. She played a little with Katak and swept the floor but all the time she was watching out for the others to arrive. Then she spotted them. Throwing down her broom, she ran up the road towards them.

CHAPTER 3

Xin-Hui, Joseph and Vinod arrived at the kampong together. The holidays had started and if they had been unable to help Yusof look after his sick creatures they would have been bored already. As it was, they were looking forward to working on the rescue centre and building new safe areas for the creatures.

They spotted Faradilla running towards them. Jumping up and down with impatience

"Hurry! Hurry!" she called excitedly. "Ibrahim's got something important to tell us."

The children broke into a run and in no time at all they were sitting cross-legged in a circle on the anjung of Ibrahim's house, which is where they always had their meetings. Ibrahim was alert and twinkling.

"Well, Tunku sent Number One Son to find Matahari because he wanted a meeting with him. Something was wrong in the forest and

Bapa thought the head man would know what the problem was. So Bapa and I went to the Orang Asli village in the forest. We stayed there overnight." Ibrahim blurted out. He was talking so quickly, his tongue was tripping over itself.

"Oooh, you did not!" "Were you frightened?"

"What is wrong in the forest?"

"Do they really hang shrunken heads on poles outside their doors?"

"No, of course they do not!" Ibrahim answered testily. "Now, listen, or I shall not tell you." He was feeling rather important.

"The head man said that Matahari and Tunku would have their meeting in the glade and that he would go and I could go with him. So we stayed in the village overnight and the next day the head man and I set off for the glade. We got there at dusk."

"You lucky beggar!" "Were you scared?"

"Why did you not take me?"

They all knew by now of this legendary meeting place for the forest creatures, but Ibrahim and Joseph were the only humans - apart from the Orang Asli - who had ever been there.

"No! No! You must listen. This is important. I know what we can do in the holidays," Ibrahim interrupted.

"But we have not gone through the emails yet. Did you choose one on your own?" the practical Xin-Hui wondered.

"No, it is not from one of the emails. They will have to wait until later. This is really urgent. Listen to me. That night in the glade we waited for a long time. Matahari arrived first, then Tunku, and then Hitam Malam. Hitam Malam was very upset." Ibrahim paused, catching his breath. He glanced around at the children's expectant faces before continuing.

"Bear cubs are being taken from the forest, from their mothers. Two bears have already been killed and their cubs taken – by humans! And now another five cubs have been taken. The mothers were either netted or fell into the old bear pits. So – that is nine cubs taken. Hitam Malam is desperate for help in finding the cubs."

The children gasped in horror.

"Why would they take the bear cubs?" cried Faradilla.

Ibrahim did not tell her what he had heard. He knew she would get too upset. "What matters is that we need to get them back," he stated firmly.

"How can we do that?"

"Tunku's organised the gibbons - the forest scouts - and the macaques to file out and find the cubs. They are so nosey, they will find anything in the forest. As soon as they find them, word will spread in no time and we shall at least know where they are. Then we can make our plans."

"Well said, Ibrahim" exclaimed Joseph. "Who do you think could have taken them? Why are they taking them?"

"That is what we shall have to find out. And then we shall have to rescue them." Vinod was ecstatic 'A project at last!' He had known all along that they would find something to do.

"What can we do while we are waiting for the gibbons to return?" asked Xin-Hui. "They should be back some time today with news. Come on, we cannot do anything until then, so let's go and help Bapa build some more pens."

Ibrahim was right. The children filed down to the sanctuary Yusof had started building for sick forest creatures. In time, it would be a splendid sanctuary, where people would come and pay to see the creatures, they would learn about them, and the money raised would then be used to help protect the forest. They already had about fifty creatures there who had been too badly burned in the great fire to be returned to the forest, or who were just too old to fend for themselves. They needed a lot of looking after, so there were always jobs for the children to do. They worked solidly for a few hours.

The girls, as usual, washed and filled up water bowls and feeding bowls. The boys repaired pens and cleaned out dirty bedding, replacing it with fresh straw, wood chips, or whatever else was required. But the work did not take their minds off the potential project they had in mind. All of them were thinking furiously as they worked.

A small macaque in the treetops threw a nut at Ibrahim, which hit him on the head. He looked up, and listened to the monkey. The children were accustomed to Ibrahim's ability to communicate with wild animals.

"What did he say?" asked Joseph.

"He says that all the monkey tribes have scoured the forest, and there is no sign of the stolen bear cubs anywhere. But," he added ominously, "some men were seen two days ago, heading north and carrying cages."

"We must go and find them," cried Faradilla. "It has got to be them."

"Well, it will take us some time to get there. The forest is very big, and very wet right now. And I do not think our parents will let us go off for all that time on our own."

"Maybe we can square it with the parents. This could be news. What if Shirley Pooper and Bert were to come with us? It might be another scoop for them. The parents will surely be alright if we have grown-ups with us. And I've got a tent and camping gear at home." Joseph was getting quite excited at the prospect of camping in the forest.

"What an adventure!" Vinod was jumping up and down gleefully.

"Ugh. There will be leeches and ants and creepy crawlies - and **SNAKES** – everywhere." Xin-Hui shuddered. She was still not fully at home in the forest. "I do not think my parents will agree."

Yusof who had gone off to take a telephone call, came over to the children.

"Professor Profundo just called," he explained. He and Toby are coming for the summer. They will be arriving tomorrow."

"Great!" yelled the children, punching the air with their fists. They liked the Professor, he was fun. And they especially liked Toby.

"Yusof, we want to go into the forest and look for the missing bear cubs. I'm sure we can find them. I've got a tent and camping equipment. I thought maybe we could take Shirley Pooper and Bert with us. They're grown ups and if they come too the parents probably won't object. Would you allow us?" The words just tumbled out. Joseph was sure Yusof would agree.

But Yusof was thoughtful. If the children found the men who had taken the cubs, it could be very dangerous.

"I need to think about this," he said. "Give me until tomorrow, and I shall tell you what I believe you should do."

Professor Profundo and Toby drew up in a rattly old taxi which had chugged and puffed its way down the bumpy road through the kampong to the last house, which was Yusof's. Aishah ran down the steps to greet them, she was particularly fond of Professor Profundo. She gave them both a big hug. In their honour, she had prepared a veritable feast and all the children were invited. Yusof, Aishah, and the Professor were talking non-stop, as were the children. They had so much to tell each other.

The Professor told Yusof that this time, he really wanted to go into the forest and find more pitcher plants. His research into the Rafflesia had been very successful and he had written an erudite paper on it which was clearly due to the fact that he had been able to do so much research in the forest itself. He was bubbling with enthusiasm.

"Oh, Marjorie sent you this," he said to Aishah, drawing out two large pots of home-made strawberry jam from his rucksack. "She says no strawberries taste better than those grown in our own garden. I have to say I'm very partial to Marjorie's strawberry jam." He chuckled as he contemplated the contents of the jars.

"Thank-you, Professor," Aishah answered. "Tell Marjorie her jam is excellent, but I would much prefer to see her."

"Ah, you know how she hates flying. She would have to be anaesthetised to get her on to an aeroplane. She says perhaps you could visit us in England one day. How many years is it since you two last saw each other? It must be nearly twenty. Goodness, how time flies!"

It was Aishah's turn to chuckle. "Then, definitely, we must come to visit you in England, Professor," she replied.

The children drew Toby off to the padang where they could chatter among themselves, away from the grown-ups.

"What are we going to do this holiday?" Toby asked eagerly. He was sure there would be something exciting to do.

"Well! You tell him, Ibrahim" said Joseph, as the others started talking all at once. Ibrahim explained everything again to Toby whose eyes grew bigger and bigger as he listened to Ibrahim.

"Wow!" he said finally. "I just knew something exciting would be going on. What are we going to do about it?"

"The monkey told Ibrahim that they cannot find the cubs anywhere in the forest, so they must have been taken out already," added Joseph, perplexed. But the question is where?"

"We know that some men were seen travelling north, carrying cages. We know that four sets of cubs have been taken. Maybe they will come back for more, lah!" Xin-Hui gave vent to a thought which had not crossed any of their minds.

"Oh no! cried Vinod, horrified. "You are right. They probably will come back."

"If they do, the creatures will be on the look-out for them and so will the Orang-Asli," commented Ibrahim. "But the creatures will not leave the forest. It is too dangerous for them. I think we should try to help but we need to go into the forest for several days and I do not see how your parents will allow us to go off on our own for that long."

Joseph sat still thinking for a minute, then looked up, grinning. " I thought we might ask Shirley Pooper and Bert to come with us, but I don't think the parents will have much confidence in them," Joseph was thinking hard again.

The children laughed. Shirley Pooper and Bert were always getting into scrapes.

"I've got it!" Toby exclaimed. "What if my Dad comes with us? I know he wants to work on pitcher plants but he loves a good adventure. He could keep an eye on us and work on his pitcher plants at the same time."

"Do you think he would?" asked Joseph, brightening up at once. Professor Profundo was highly regarded by everybody. Surely the parents would allow their children to go with the eminent Professor Profundo.

"Let us go and ask him," cried Faradilla jumping up excitedly.

"Hang on. It's not just the Professor. We have to ask all the parents," cautioned Joseph.

"We can start with the Professor," said Ibrahim. "And if he says yes, then we can ask Bapa to call a meeting with all the parents."

"I think mine will need a lot of persuasion," said Xin-Hui, still shuddering at the prospect of staying overnight in the forest. But she was determined not to be left out.

The children made their way from the padang back to Yusof's house where Toby put their idea to his father.

"Oh, What a splendid idea! What an adventure!" the Professor cried. "And if we find those cubs, what a wonderful thing that will be."

"You mean you will come with us?" said Joseph, hardly able to believe his ears.

"My dear boy, I would not miss this for all the world, although I don't think it will be quite such a big adventure as our last one, eh?" He winked at Joseph, his big bushy eyebrow waggling.

But Yusof was still doubtful. "These men will undoubtedly be very dangerous. They may be armed."

"My Dear Yusof, if these children can defeat the evil palm oil baron, they can defeat anybody!" cried the Professor. "What do you say, children?" He turned towards them, smiling broadly.

"Yes!" they chorused excitedly. They had a pretty good idea the Professor would support them, but this was terrific. Vinod did a little dance in his excitement, and Xin-Hui and Faradilla clapped their hands. The three bigger boys just grinned.

"Besides, You've told me often enough that Ibrahim has a special affinity with the wild animals and they will never hurt the children. Indeed, the children will always be protected in the forest by the creatures and by the Orang-Asli. Is that right?" he asked, looking directly at Yusof.

Yusof grudgingly agreed, wondering how he would explain this to the other parents. Aishah intervened. "Maybe they can go but we shall have to do a lot of explaining to the other parents. I propose we ask them here this evening and we can have a meeting."

"Ibu, thank-you." Cried Faradilla throwing her arms around her mother and giving her a big kiss. Aishah laughed and gave her daughter a hug.

The parents arrived for the meeting on time. They knew something was afoot as their children had been very excited, bubbling with energy for the past couple of days. All the parents had considerable respect for Yusof and Professor Profundo and had infinite faith in both of them.

When they had all settled down, Professor Profundo explained that he was going into the forest to conduct research into the behaviour of pitcher plants. Somehow, he omitted to say anything about the stolen bear cubs. He told the parents he thought it would be a good idea for the children to accompany him for a few days. Not only would they would learn a great deal about the forest but it would keep them out of mischief.

Mr and Mrs Brown were the most pragmatic of the parents, partly because Joseph was older than the others, and partly because they had become deeply involved with Yusof and Aishah in the running of the animal sanctuary which they had helped establish as a charity and for which they helped raise funds. They were pleased that Joseph would have something useful to do in the holidays.

Mr and Mrs Singh too were anxious for Vinod to be meaningfully occupied during the holidays. Mrs Singh was very conscious that she was very busy with his baby brother and therefore did not have as much time as she would have liked for Vinod. Mr Singh was concerned that whatever Vinod became involved in, it should be a noble and fitting pursuit for a young Sikh and, of course, that he should be safe. In Professor Profundo's hands, what could go wrong?

Mr and Mrs Chan, until the great fight, had had no experience of the forest and were still in awe of it. They were city folk and they were terrified for the safety of their precious only daughter, Xin-Hui.

"But, Mummee, Daddee," Xin-Hui pleaded "you know the creatures now. You liked Cahaya Bulan. She will always look after me. I am not afraid, not at all. No harm will come to any of us, not with the Professor." She did not admit how terrified she was of the creepy-crawlies and the snakes.

Every time she thought of Cahaya Bulan, Mrs Chan grew misty-eyed. She had made friends with Cahaya Bulan when they were digging the fire-break before the great fight, and felt the experience she had shared with that exquisite beast had been, well, mystical. It was as if the great fight had been a beautiful dream, but it was real. Mr Chan listened quietly, leaning his head slightly to one side.

"Very well, Xin-Hui," he said finally. "But you must keep your hand-phone with you at all times and call your mother every evening."

"That's an excellent idea. I give you my personal guarantee that Xin-Hui will do that," said Professsor Profundo hastily. So far, so good. He did not want the parents to change their minds.

"That is a sensible idea. In that case, if Vinod telephones us every evening he, too, can go," Mr Singh said.

Mr Brown raised his hands and shrugged. "I see no harm in it. Actually, I think it is an excellent idea."

The parents departed, content in the knowledge that their children would be fittingly occupied during the holidays.

Yusof looked at the Professor. "Professor, you said nothing about the bear cubs."

Oh dear, I completely forgot," said the Professor. "How remiss of me. You know, I seem to be getting more and more absent-minded these days." He scratched his head ruefully.

Yusof grinned at his friend. "Sometimes you are a wicked old man. But you could be in danger."

"Come, now, Yusof. Where is your faith? There will be no danger for us in the forest. There is far more danger out here, in the kampongs, in the city."

"I am afraid you are right, my friend," Yusof replied, patting him on the shoulder.

Trussed up in rattan nets

CHAPTER 4

The children had gathered on the padang.
It was early in the morning. Aishah had
provided a filling breakfast of roti prata and
they had all their gear with them. Joseph
and Toby would share one tent, Ibrahim and
Vinod another, Xin-Hui and Faradilla would
share a third, and Professor Profundo was
to have a tent all to himself. They had food
and water flasks, a tin plate, a tin mug, and
a spoon each, a compass, and a map of the
forest - such as it was, as the forest was
largely uncharted. They each had a change
of clothes, a sleeping bag, and a large towel.
They all had their hand-phones with them,
fully charged, and turned off to preserve the
batteries. They would only be turned on for
calls home or for emergencies. And they each
carried a torch. The boys and the Professor
each wore watches and they all wore walking

boots and long trousers tucked in – to keep the leeches out. Yusof had carved a large stave for the Professor, and five smaller ones for the children, to assist them in walking along wet and slippery paths. It was the monsoon season after all.

Joseph had ensured that, for self defence, each of the children carried a catapult and a collection of small stones.

They were ready. Lifting their rucksacks on to their backs, they took their leave of the parents, all of whom had gathered to see them off. Hugs and kisses all round and they set off, walking single file along the narrow forest trail.

The parents, standing forlornly on the padang, waved long after the children were out of sight. Aishah rallied them and poured lashings of piping hot coffee.

"They will be fine," she laughed. "There is absolutely nothing to worry about." Mrs Chan, full of hot coffee and sweet biscuits, was already feeling a lot better. "Of course" she said, smiling sweetly.

Professor Profundo and the children plodded along the trail in the cool of the early morning. It was wet, dripping, slippery mud underfoot. Vapour was still rising off the ground. They found their staves very helpful.

"Where are we going, Professor?" Joseph asked. They had not had a chance to discuss their direction, or anything else for that matter, preparations for their departure had been made in such haste.

"Why, North, of course" said the Professor. "We need to find out what is happening to those bear cubs."

"But I thought....."

"Ah yes, the pitcher plants! That was a red herring for your parents. Hope you don't mind!"

'Wow! The Professor is so cool!' Vinod was impressed.

Xin-Hui and Faradilla looked at each other and giggled and Joseph, Toby and Ibrahim were grinning like Cheshire cats.

They plodded on doggedly for more than an hour. All around them an army of small creatures was keeping watch, passing on word of their passage, in the undergrowth, in the treetops, they were everywhere, but largely unseen. Occasionally the children spotted a monkey, a squirrel, or a snake hanging from a tree. They stopped for a rest. The Professor consulted his compass and the map and then they continued onwards, deeper into the forest. Xin-Hui and Vinod had never been so deeply into the forest before. Scrutinizing everything, they kept looking over their shoulders, certain that they were being followed. Instinctively the children bunched up close together. Any one of them left trailing scampered to catch up.

As the sun rose, its watery rays burst through the thick canopy of tree tops warming the ground, warming the bushes and leaves. Great bursts of steam and vapour rose into the atmosphere.

"It is like a Sauna in here." Xin-Hui exclaimed.

They walked all day, stopping regularly for rests. In that time they saw no-one and caught only a few fleeting glimpses of creatures. But they heard sounds all around them all the time, cicadas calling, twigs snapping, big plops of rain dropping, branches creaking, birds, monkeys, and all manner of other creatures calling. The forest was never silent or still. Faradilla was very tired, her leg was hurting, and she was limping heavily.

"At the next dry clearing we come to, we stop and make camp," the Professor finally announced.

The children were relieved. They were all tired and hungry. Another half hour's march and they entered a little clearing, dry, sheltered, and just big enough to pitch their four tents with space to spare for a camp fire. In no time at all they had pitched their tents and rolled out their sleeping bags.

Professor Profundo sent the boys off to collect dry twigs to make a small camp-fire. He set the girls to collect water off the leaves and bushes, so that they could boil some rice and make a cup of tea. Meanwhile, just in case, he got out an old primus stove which he had carefully packed. He pulled out three tins of baked beans, and half a dozen apples.

Soon enough the boys came back with twigs, and the girls returned with water. They managed to light the fire with the twigs which were dry because they had been buried deep under a pile of leaves. They boiled rice in coconut milk, and heated up the tins of baked beans. When the food was cooked, they ate heartily. They had hot tea with lashings of sugar. Then they ate their apples, after which everyone was full and felt a lot better.

The Professor rooted around in his rucksack, found the map and spread it out on his lap. "I think we must be about here," he said, stabbing at the map with his finger. "This is the northern part of the forest," – circling a large area – "but you can see how big it is and it is uncharted. My concern is that we do not know where the trails might be nor do we know which of those trails the men might have taken. I do not think we can make any decision as to which direction we go in until we get there. There may be some clues!" He grinned at them. "This is so exciting!"

"Tomorrow is another day," he said, folding away the map. "I think we should all get an early night now. Whilst in the forest, we should rise with the sun and go to bed when darkness sets in."

The light of the campfire had deceived them all. Looking over her shoulder, Xin-Hui shivered to see how dark the forest had become, and she could see the forms of large bats flitting through the trees. The children quickly scampered into their tents and into their sleeping bags. They were lying on hard ground without pillows but that did not matter. Xin-Hui reached out her hand to Faradilla.

"Faradilla, are you there?" she whispered.

"Yes, I am," whispered Faradilla. Very soon they were fast asleep. " Joseph, this is great!" whispered Toby.

Still sitting by the dying embers of the camp fire, Professor Profundo hummed quietly to himself. *'This is the life!'* He drew out of his pocket a small pewter flask. Unscrewing the cap, he took a swig – for medicinal purposes, to keep the chill of the night from his bones!

He, too, retired to his tent. *'Well, there have been no mishaps today. I think Yusof may have exaggerated the dangers a little.'* Then he was snoring gently, like a baby.

While they slept there were visitors to the camp. Rats came and gobbled up any remnants of food which had been spilled and a porcupine slowly shuffled through. Berminyak, the snake, slithered silently into the camp visiting each of the children in their tents, sniffing out their warmth with his forked tongue. He visited Professor Profundo who groaned and turned over in his sleep. Berminyak removed himself speedily and silently. He knew they were here, that was enough for the time being. But he wanted to know. What did they want? What were they doing deep in the forest? They had no place here. Berminyak did not have a nice temperament, and he resented outsiders. There were other visitors to the camp too.

When the children woke in the morning, they found two fresh, ripe mangoes outside each tent. They made a good breakfast, but where had they come from? The fire had been built up with fresh twigs, and the saucepan had been filled with fresh water, so they could have tea. The Professor denied all knowledge of these niceties. He was just as mystified as the children were.

After breakfast they broke camp and set off again. A long march lay ahead of them. The Professor had his compass in his hand all the time, constantly checking it. The day was much the same as the previous day except that it rained for hours, hampering their progress. They were wet, damp and soggy.

"Even my knickers are wet," grumbled Xin-Hui, as she tried to wring out her hair. "Yuk, these leeches are a nuisance." Vinod was getting adept at pulling them off. "Yeah, I got one on my neck, would you believe!" said Joseph.

"And I'm covered in mosquito bites." Toby slapped his ear.

"Well, I've got something for that," said the Professor. "Here, spray this on to all your exposed bits." He handed Toby a can of spray. Gratefully Toby sprayed himself and passed it on to Joseph, who passed it on yet again, until they had all sprayed themselves with anti- mosquito spray.

They had reached the edge of the northern part of the forest.

"Now where? "the Professor asked himself. He thought for a while.

"There are two paths here, boys. I propose that we set up one tent – for the girls, so they can rest and you boys take one path and I take the other. We shall give ourselves an hour to get back here, to the girls. What do you think?"

The boys agreed. So they pitched the girls' tent and left them sitting quietly in it.

"Change your clothes and dry out," the Professor told them, "and don't worry. We shall be back before you can say Jack Robinson." He left them some biscuits and some water.

"Synchronise watches!" the Professor commanded the boys. He gave them a roll of gardening string and a pair of scissors. "Tie pieces of the string to trees and branches to mark your way in case you get lost," he said. "Now, you take that path and I shall take this one."

"Don't forget, if you find anything untoward do not try to be heroes. Come straight back, and we shall decide what to do together. Understood?"

The boys nodded in agreement. They set off, Joseph and Ibrahim leading the way, Toby and Vinod following closely behind. The Professor, brandishing his stout stave, strode off in the other direction.

As soon as they were left alone, the girls wriggled out of their wet clothing, dried themselves off, and put on dry things. They felt a lot better. They hung their damp things up to dry.

"I do not think they will dry, they are so wet," Xin-Hui said.

"We can try. They cannot get any wetter," Faradilla answered her, munching a biscuit. "Have you noticed how quiet it is? There is no sound in this part of the forest."

Xin-Hui listened.

"You are right. I cannot hear anything, not even the cicadas. That is very strange." She shivered. "I am scared being here on our own."

"You have got me with you," Faradilla answered her matter-of-factly.

The girls worked their way through a whole packet of biscuits. They chatted for a while and then ran out of things to say, so they sat in silence listening to the forest. All they could hear was the drip, drip of rain water and in the silence every sound seemed to be exaggerated. They climbed into their sleeping bags and lay on the ground side by side. There was a rustling noise outside, then another, closer, something was rubbing against the tent. They froze in horror, watching something creep along the bottom towards the entrance.

"Faradilla," Xin-Hui was so scared, she could scarcely whisper. "What?"

"What is it?"

"I do not know. It is not very big."

"Aaah!" Xin-Hui gasped, grabbing hold of Faradilla. The girls sat, clinging to each other, watching the moving thing. They did not dare move. There was a rustling and scraping at the front of the tent. Suddenly, at the entrance, a little furry head popped through, big round unblinking eyes looking at them in wonder. The girls relaxed and laughed at themselves. It was a baby monkey.

"What are you doing here? Where is your Mummy?" asked Faradilla. The monkey ran over to her and, jumping up, clung on to her as hard as it could. It snuggled itself into her. Laughing, she cuddled it.

"It is alright. You have nothing to be frightened of," she said. Xin-Hui gave it a biscuit. The baby monkey ate hungrily.

"It says its Mummy was frightened by bad men who passed through here two days ago. They had guns. In the panic this little monkey got lost. He cannot find his Mummy." Faradilla had her brother's gift for communicating with the animals.

"Never mind," said Xin-Hui, charmed by the little fellow. "We shall look after you." The girls settled down happily with the baby monkey between them.

Professor Profundo plodded along his chosen path. *'Nothing here! Nothing at all.'* He continued for half an hour but it was clear that nobody had passed down this path for a very long time. After half an hour he had to turn back. He reached the girls' tent precisely on the hour.

They showed him the baby monkey. They had been so absorbed with it that they had forgotten they were all alone and frightened.

The boys did not return. The Professor and the girls waited an hour. Then the Professor went off again down the other path to try and find them. There was no sign of the boys. He was getting worried. Darkness descended. He could not go on. It was now pitch dark and the girls would be frightened. He returned to their tent. He pitched his own alongside, although it was difficult in the dark. They could not cook tonight so he pulled out biscuits and cheese and opened another can of baked beans. Cold beans are just as good as hot beans when you are hungry.

The baby monkey appreciated everything. Xin-Hui was frightened.

"What has happened to the boys? It is so dark. They will be frightened. Do you think they are hurt? We should go and look for them."

"No," said the Professor. "They are sensible boys and will be able to look after themselves. We shall wait 'till the morning and then go and find them."

"The Professor is right, Xin-Hui," Faradilla said. "And Ibrahim knows the forest very well. I am not concerned for him and he will look after the others, although I think they will be hungry." She spoke quietly, her faith in her brother absolute.

They went to bed having scarcely eaten. None of them was hungry. Neither did they sleep well. Despite what they said, both the Professor and Faradilla were just as worried about the boys as Xin-Hui. They rose at dawn the next day, broke camp, and ate quickly. Then they set off down the path the boys had taken. The little monkey clung limpet-like to Faradilla. It had rained heavily in the night and the ground was muddy and slippery. Without their staves the girls would not have made it but they struggled on. Nothing would stop them from finding the boys.

"Look, there's a piece of string," Faradillla cried. She had spotted it tied to a tree branch. Xin-Hui found another, and then another. "They were here then." Encouraged, they pressed on more quickly.

"I hear voices! Ssshh!" Faradilla lifted her finger to her lips. Xin-Hui and the Professor froze and listened intently. Sure enough, they heard voices too.

"It's Ibrahim. He's calling for help." said Faradilla, breaking into a run. Xin-Hui and the Professor followed her, breathing heavily. The shouts were getting louder, closer. There were more voices than just Ibrahim's. *'Thank-you, God.'* the Professor was greatly relieved. The shouting got louder as they drew nearer. Rounding a bend in the path, they stopped in their tracks, mouths open in disbelief. There were the boys, all four of them, trussed up in rattan nets hanging high above the ground from a tree.

"What are you doing up there?"

"What do you think we are doing up here? Get us down, Silly. We were trapped. We've been here all night, and we are cold and hungry. And we are very uncomfortable."

"There must be a counter-balance to their weight. Look around," ordered Professor Profundo. He was rooting about in the bushes. "Aah, here it is!" he cried triumphantly. A long liana was attached to a heavy branch on the ground. Huffing and puffing, he gradually lifted up the weighty branch. As he did so the boys' prisons slowly lowered. The Professor untied the liana, holding on to it with all his might.

"I have to let go, boys. And you'll come down very quickly, bend your knees for the impact,"

he called. And he let the liana go.

The boys plummeted to earth. Initially they just rolled about on the ground, then they managed to extricate themselves and stand up rubbing the circulation back into their legs and feet..

"It was horrible up there all night. It was wet and cold, it poured with rain, and so dark!

Very scary!" Toby said, giving his father a big hug. "Thanks, Dad. We were getting hungry."

Joseph, Ibrahim, and Vinod, shivering in their boots, were equally grateful to the Professor. "We were just following the path when we were hauled up. It all happened so quickly, we did not see the nets at all."

"We were not supposed to see them. They were well camouflaged," said Ibrahim.

"Why did you not telephone us?" Xin-Hui demanded. "You all have your handphones." "How could we have got at them, all trussed up as we were?" Joseph thought Xin-Hui was being unusually silly.

"Come on. Let's get off this path," said Professor Profundo, striking off into the forest. They fought their way through the undergrowth for a while until they found a small clearing.

"Let's have a rest here," said the Professor. The children collapsed in an exhausted heap. "Now, boys, tell us what happened." He pulled out biscuits and cheese from his rucksack. He did not dare light a fire here. It was too close to the path. "Here. Eat!" The boys chomped hungrily on their biscuits and cheese. And for a while there was silence.

Joseph was the first to finish.

"We were walking along, just as you told us, tying string to branches and things when we came round the bend and – whoosh – there we were up in the air. We shouted and shouted until we were hoarse, but nobody heard us."

"That is strange" said Ibrahim, "because usually there are creatures all around us but, if you listen, there is hardly any sound here. And no creature came to our calls. It is as if they have deserted this part of the forest."

They stopped to listen. Ibrahim was right. There was scarcely any sound coming from the forest.

Ibrahim caught sight of the little monkey clinging to Faradilla. "Where did he come from?"

"He lost his Mummy when they were running away from the bad men two days ago." "What bad men?" Joseph raised his head.

"He says they were coming along this path. They were carrying guns."

Gently Ibrahim prised the little monkey's fingers off Faradilla's teeshirt. He stroked the little fellow, and talked to him.

Eventually, he said "There were four men, with guns, carrying cages. He thinks the bear cubs may have been in there. He says the men stopped to put up those net traps because bears use this path. Well, they used to but they do not any more because they are frightened. He says his Mummy and others of his tribe helped a bear to escape one of these nets by chewing through the fronds with her teeth. Hitam Malam said that had happened. They stole her cubs while she was in the net. He says that all the creatures have left this part of the forest because of the bad men."

"They will be back to see whether their traps worked. If they do come back I think it will be in daylight. It will be too dark at night." Joseph was thinking out loud. If they come back, Ibrahim, perhaps you and I could follow them and see where they go."

"You're not leaving me out" said Toby. "Nor me." said Vinod.

"We must think this through. If we do find the bear cubs, what then? How will we get them back?"

"We shall need help," said Ibrahim. "I shall have to go and find Tunku or Matahari or someone. Maybe I could find the head man of the Orang Asli."

"You can't go on your own."

"Why not? I know the forest better than anyone and you need to watch these nets in case the bad men come back. Besides, I can travel faster on my own."

They could not fault Ibrahim's logic. So it was agreed that Ibrahim would set off to find help while Joseph, Toby and Vinod stayed to watch the nets and look out for the bad men should they return. They would hide in the undergrowth, taking turns to take watches.

"What shall we do if they do come back?" Vinod asked hesitantly. "We shall have to follow them and find out where they go."

"We can't all follow them. They will see us."

"No. Just you two and me," said Joseph. "The Professor and the girls will have to stay here so that we know where to meet up again and Ibrahim can come back here with help."

"Well" said the Professor "that makes sense to me. But we should pitch our camp somewhere else, away from this path. We do not want anyone to find us. Moreover," he said gleefully " I think I spotted a cluster of very fine Nepenthes Rajah just over there." He pointed to a dense patch of forest about five hundred yards away.

"Perhaps I could study the plants while we wait. The girls can help me."

"What is Nepenthes Rajah?" asked Xin-Hui who was quite happy to stay with Professor

Profundo. She did not fancy lying low in undergrowth, getting soaked, being bitten by lots of creepy crawlies and torn by thorns. Faradilla would have liked to join the boys but she would not be able to keep up with them.

"Ah, it is one of the largest pitcher plants. It is said that one was once found with two and a half litres of fluid in it and it was digesting a drowned rat in the fluid."

"What! A plant which holds liquid in it?" Vinod was disbelieving.

"Yes. That's why it is called a Pitcher Plant. It's flower is shaped like a pitcher to hold the liquid." Professor Profundo was a very patient man.

Ugh!" said Xin-Hui and Faradilla unanimously. Perhaps helping the Professor was not such a good idea, after all.

They got up and headed towards the patch of forest the Professor had pointed out. After searching around for some time they found a small clearing hidden behind some very dense undergrowth. If they pitched camp here they would not be seen from either of the pathways. They would even be able to light a campfire and it would not be seen. The children set about clearing their little space in the forest. They pitched tents for Professor Profundo, the girls, and Vinod, Toby and Joseph. Ibrahim needed a tent of his own so the other three boys would have to squeeze in together. Then they got a fire going and they all ate a cooked meal before Ibrahim set off on his own with his rucksack on his back, clutching a compass, deep into the forest. He looked very small as he melted into its density.

"Are you sure you know where you are going?" "Be careful."

"Come back soon." The other children called.

Vinod was sent off to keep the first watch over the abandoned nets. Should he see the men coming he would immediately return to fetch Joseph and Toby. Coming close to the nets on the pathway he found a good observation point and lay down in a cluster of long grasses and ferns. Luckily they were dry. It was really very comfortable and before long he was snoozing gently.

Joseph and Toby were helping the Professor and the girls. Professor Profundo was delighted to have found these particular pitcher plants.

"See how big they are!" His enthusiasm was infectious. "They trap insects mainly but sometimes small rodents too. And then they digest them slowly. This liquid here is their digestive juice. Basically, whatever they catch is melted down into a sort of soup."

"Yuk! How disgusting!" Xin-Hui could not believe her ears.

Joseph thought it was time he relieved Vinod. Off he went to find him but Vinod was still snoozing in the long grass. Joseph searched around for some time before he almost tripped over Vinod's comatose body.

Vinod, wake up. Did you see anything?"

Just as Vinod was about to answer him, Joseph dropped to the ground beside him. "Sshhh! Don't say a word." He whispered.

The boys lay on the ground still as sticks. Two men were coming along the footpath from the opposite direction.

"Ah, look! We caught something, but it got away."

The boys could hardly breath. *'They are talking about us.'*

"Hmph. We shall have to try again. The Fat Superintendent will be very angry if we do not bring back more cubs."

They set to work burying the nets under a pile of leaves, disguising them and setting the trigger to the trap. Their work done, they returned in the direction from where they had come.

"I am going to follow them" whispered Joseph. "You go back and fetch Toby, then catch me up. Don't get caught in the nets. Hurry!"

Vinod scrambled to his feet and scampered off to fetch Toby. Joseph waited until the men were round the bend before he released the trap, then set off after them making sure he kept as close to the undergrowth as possible so that he could dive in if necessary. The men did not seem to be in a hurry which made it easy, a little later, for Vinod and Toby to catch up with Joseph.

"What's happening?" whispered Toby.

"Nothing yet. They're just ambling along. It's almost as if they don't want to go back." The boys followed the two men for some time without incident until they broke out of the forest. Little did they know that they, in turn, were being followed. Berminyak the snake was curious as to what these children were doing in this part of the forest and he was very nosey. Slithering silently along, keeping to the shadows, nobody was aware of his presence.

Then suddenly the forest ended. In front of them right up to the edge of the forest lay a palm oil plantation as far as the eye could see. A small dirt road ran between the forest and the plantation. The men ambled on down this road.

"No, no, stay here in the forest" whispered Joseph as Vinod was about to follow the men still further. "We'll be seen. Where are they going? Just watch."

The boys watched the men disappear into the distance.

"I'm going after them. You two stay here and wait for me." Joseph said.

"No. I should go." Vinod pulled Joseph's arm. "You are white, and I am brown. If they see me, it will not be so unusual for a brown boy to be on the path. But a white boy! You would not stand a chance. Besides, if I stay off the road I can hide behind the palm oil trees as I go." Vinod was right.

"O.K., but be very careful." Joseph admonished him. "Check watches and make sure you are back within two hours. If you are not we shall come and find you."

CHAPTER 5

Ibrahim was finding it tough trekking through the forest. It was very, very dense, wet and soggy. It started to rain again and he was quickly soaked. All he could hear was the rolling thunder, the sound of rain drumming on leaves and the plop plop of drips. Through the branches of the trees he could see lightning flashing overhead. The ground was slippery underfoot and it was difficult to follow any path or trail. He was grateful that Professor Profundo had given him the compass. Although he knew large tracts of the forest very well he was not familiar with this section and, besides, before there had always been creatures to help when he needed them. But now there were no creatures. *It's very spooky here. I wish I could find Tunku.'* . he thought, feeling tired.

"Tunku," he called, every few metres. But there was no response. He trudged on, calling again and again. It was getting dark and Ibrahim was exhausted. Climbing a tree he found a dry, comfortable place to rest with his back against the trunk. He took an apple and a lump of cheese from his pocket and ate hungrily. He licked water off the leaves. He would have to stay here for the night but it would be safe enough. He fell asleep. It was not really that comfortable sleeping in a sitting position in a tree, so Ibrahim slept fitfully, waking frequently only to regret his waking. He was cold, wet, and hungry. He tried to get back to sleep again as quickly as possible.

Finally it was dawn. He could see through the trees. Shinning stiffly down the trunk of the tree, Ibrahim stretched and rubbed his aching limbs. Then he set off again, calling as he went: "Tunku. Tunku. Tunku!" His progress was slow, hampered by the slippery, wet undergrowth. His legs were weakening and his tummy rumbled incessantly. "Oh, Tunku, where are you?" he wondered. Suddenly, his legs shot out from under him as he slipped down an incline. He sat despondently at the bottom, head in his arms. He had been silly to boast that he knew the forest. Where was he? Where were the creatures? He wiped away a large tear. *'I am not going to cry but I am so tired.'* He lay down on his side curled up in a ball and slept.

Someone was shaking him. "Go away," he muttered.

He felt someone shaking him again. Reluctantly Ibrahim opened his eyes and looked up. His face lit up with a huge smile.

"Number One Son!" he exclaimed. "I am so glad to see you! Where have all the creatures gone? This part of the forest is empty."

He quickly explained to Number One Son that he was searching for Tunku, and that they were hoping to rescue the bear cubs. Number One Son told Ibrahim to stay and rest. He, Number One Son, would fetch Tunku immediately and they would return in a very short time, so Ibrahim waited.

Tunku returned with Number One Son and listened to Ibrahim's story. Tunku told Ibrahim that the creatures had left that part of the forest because they were frightened of the bad men. He, Tunku, and Number One Son would go with Ibrahim back to the other children and find out what was happening. With his long arms, Tunku swung Ibrahim up on to his back and they set off, climbing trees, sailing through the forest canopy. Ibrahim, in his element, forgot all his woes.

They reached the camp where Professor Profundo, wholly engrossed in his work, was waxing lyrical about the Nepenthes Rajah he had found. The girls told Ibrahim that the other boys had gone off after the bad men to see where they were going. Tunku decided it was time for the creatures to return to this part of the forest. He sent Number One Son off to find Matahari and Hitam Malam and bring them here, to the Professor's camp. Tunku and Ibrahim then set off to catch up with the other boys.

Following the path, Ibrahim showed Tunku the net traps. They untied the nets from the trigger log so that they would not trap anybody before moving on. Eventually they emerged from the forest, just like Vinod, Joseph and Toby. Quickly they slipped back into the forest. They did not want to be seen.

"Look! Look, Tunku! There's Joseph," Ibrahim cried "and Toby". The boys were about three hundred yards away. Tunku and Ibrahim made their way across to the boys who were delighted to see Ibrahim again and even more delighted to see Tunku whom they had not seen since the great fight.

"Where is Vinod?"

"Oh, he has gone down the road to see where it leads. He is following two of the bad men. We are waiting for him to come back."

"Is that safe?"

"We don't know but Vinod said that as he is brown he has a better chance of not being noticed than we do. He should be back soon. We gave him two hours."

"Then we shall wait with you," said Ibrahim and Tunku, sitting down. The rain had stopped and it was getting hot so that Ibrahim's clothes were steaming. He was feeling a lot better.

Then they saw him – Vinod - running back along the road towards them. He was panting and looking back over his shoulder. Ibrahim, Joseph and Toby tensed but nobody appeared to be following Vinod.

They waved at him and he came running up. He was so out of breath that he could not speak to start with. He bent over, catching his breath.

"Take your time, Vinod".

Vinod spotted Ibrahim and Tunku. He grinned.

"So good of you to come." he said. "Let's go back, deeper into the forest. We do not want to be seen and I shall tell you all that I have observed."

They headed back until Vinod deemed it safe to stop.

"The men led me to a sort of compound, a farm maybe, but it is heavily fenced. I could hear all sorts of noises but I could not make out what they were. I made my way round the fence until I found a gap I could slip through."

"Gosh! That was brave!"

"Shut up, Toby. Inside, I was able to hide behind a small hut but I had a good view of everything. A very ugly and fat lady is in charge. I heard the men say she is the superintendent, whatever that means." Vinod took another deep breath, and sat down. "There are two very long sheds which are locked. I do not know what is inside them but there were terrible sounds coming from them – sort of crying and groaning noises. And then, at the end of the sheds, there are cages stacked up one on top of another. They are very small and the bear cubs are in those cages. There are about twenty of them. They look very uncomfortable and they are crying." Vinod wiped his arm across his face. "The whole place smells awful. I wanted to get sick. I do not know what is going on in the sheds. I could not find out. There is only a tiny hole in the bottom of one shed, otherwise the door has a big padlock on it and the Superintendent carries the keys on her belt." He paused. "I think we need to find out what is in those sheds."

None of the boys spotted Berminyak who was lying coiled in the shade alongside them.

"How are we going to find out what is in the sheds? Are you sure there is no way in?" Joseph asked. Vinod shook his head.

Ibrahim explained to Tunku all that had been said. As he did so Berminyak uncoiled himself slowly. *'There might be chickens in those sheds,'* he thought. He had been inside sheds built by humans before, all stuffed full of ripe, succulent chickens. He had had a feast. He slithered up to Tunku who regarded him with a mixture of disgust and respect. Berminyak had been known to take baby monkeys in the past.

"Great Lord of the Canopies, why should I not go and slither through that hole. I can return and tell you what I find," Berminyak suggested, waving his head from side to side, forked tongue darting constantly.

"Why are you here? And why would you do that?" Tunku asked him.

"I was curious to see these children in a forgotten part of the forest," Berminyak answered smoothly. "I was concerned for their safely."

Tunku did not believe Berminyak for one minute but he told the boys what he had offered. "Could a snake get through the hole, Vinod?" Joseph asked.

Vinod looked carefully at Berminyak. He was terrified of snakes but tried hard to hide his fear. Yes, he nodded, Berminyak would get through the hole. And so it was agreed. Berminyak would set off at once and return as soon as he could.

Keeping to the shadows and the shade, slithering between rows of palm oil trees, it did not take Berminyak long to reach the compound. He found the hole in the fence which Vinod had slipped through and rested behind the small hut, getting his bearings. He spotted the bear cubs in cages. They looked so pathetic that even he was moved. Then he spotted the long sheds. Where was the hole Vinod had mentioned? *"Aah, there it is!"* Berminyak thought, imagining the wonderful chicken dinner he was about to have. If a snake could have smiled, he would have done so. There was nobody about. Effortlessly Berminyak slithered towards the hole in the long shed and eased himself through it. It was dark inside. The noise was terrible and the smell was suffocating. He could not make it out at first. But as his eyes became accustomed to the dark, he could just make out small rusting cages, stacked one on top of another. *'Chickens!'*

Berminyak was quickly disappointed when he realized that these were not chickens at all but big creatures, black and brown. And it was these creatures who were making the noise. They were bears! Fully grown bears, squashed into tiny metal, barred cages, lying down on their sides or their backs. The cages were too small for them to stand or even sit up. The bears were so squashed that their very flesh seemed to be pouring out of the cages, between the metal bars. They all had metal tubes, some rusting, protruding from their stomachs. There was a terrible smell of rotting flesh where rusty, dirty tubes had infected the bears' stomachs. Some bears had maggots eating their flesh all around the metal tubes. The bears were crying and groaning in pain. Without exception they were holding their stomachs with their paws. Even cold-hearted Berminyak was moved. "I have entered hell!" he exclaimed. Suddenly he heard human voices outside! He must hide! Berminyak slithered into the darkest corner of the shed. Keys rattled in the lock. The bears started screaming and crying in real anguish. They rocked their cages as if desperate to escape. The bear nearest Berminyak was crying big tears. They rolled down her cheeks.

The Fat Superintendent entered, waddling on her two fat legs followed by two of the bad men Vinod had seen. Berminyak could hear the Fat Superintendent's thighs chafing as she walked; he could smell the stale sour smell of her sweat. The men approached the bear nearest to them. She started rocking and crying in her cage. They threatened her with a big iron bar and then she was quiet. They stuck a catheter onto the tube sticking out of her stomach and operated a sort of pump thing. The bear writhed in pain, chewing on her own paws until they bled. Her teeth were worn down. Berminyak saw for himself that it was because she gnawed the bars of her cage as they were milking her. The pain must be terrible for the bear. Other bears in the shed did not have metal things sticking out of them, just great holes in their abdomens and gall bladders and bile was dripping out of them. The holes were infected and bile and pus were dripping out in equal quantity. The smell was awful.

When they had finished with that bear the Fat Superintendent and the men moved on to the next bear, and then on to every bear in the shed before they left. The whole process took them two hours.

They were milking the bears for bile, but Berminyak did not know that. The Fat Superintendent and the men left the shed, locking it behind them and moved across the compound to the next shed. Berminyak could hear the weeping and wailing, for that was the noise he had originally heard, from that shed as well. Once he was sure they had gone, Berminyak emerged from his corner. He looked around at the bears, all of whom were still crying, but quietly now. Raising himself up, he announced proudly:

"I am Berminyak, descendant of the King of All Serpents."

.... the bears stirred and hesitantly at first, called from their cages, introducing themselves.

"I am Kabus Kelabu."

"I am Kulat, descendant of the Great Bear of Old." "I am No Name. I am lost to the world."

"I am Chio Bu."

"I am time itself. I have been here since time began." "I am The Forgotten One. I have been here forever"

"What do you want here, Berminyak, descendant of the King of All Serpents?' asked Kulat.

"I was curious to see what was in these sheds. There are humans in the forest who want to rescue the cubs which have been taken. Perhaps they might rescue you as well."

What had made him say that? He, cold, ruthless Berminyak who thought nothing of killing was moved to offer help to these bears.

"Aaahhh! A sigh rippled throughout the cages. "The forest is long forgotten here."

"We have no memories."

"We are the living dead. We do not exist."

And they clutched their supurating tummies with their bleeding, broken paws; they gnawed at the bars of the cages with their broken and worn teeth. They were in such great pain.

"We will see about that!" Berminyak answered. "And now I must go." He turned and slithered back through the hole in the shed.

The air outside the shed was fresh and clean after the putrid atmosphere inside. Berminyak took a deep breath. He knew he must get back to Tunku quickly. The compound was still as he slithered across it.

"A snake. A great fat snake!" the Fat Superintendent screeched. The two bad men came running up with their iron bar. Berminyak quickened his pace and made it, just in time, to the slot Vinod had squeezed through. *That was exciting!* he thought. Outside the compound he stopped to get his bearings, and then made off for the forest. He had a lot to tell.

CHAPTER 6

Berminyak and Tunku were in conference for a long time and Ibrahim was listening to them. The other boys were impatient to know what Berminyak had seen, but they had to wait. Beminyak was in no hurry. Eventually Ibrahim came over and explained everything Berminyak had said.

"Those people have created a horrible hell just for bears. Even Berminyak says it is terrible and he generally does not care about anyone or anything other than himself. The bears are suffering very much and are in great pain."

"Why?"

"I do not know."

"We must go now and rescue them," said Vinod jumping up.

"No! No! Wait! We shall need help. We cannot do this on our own."

"Right. We need to get back to the Professor. He will be anxious about us," Joseph said. "And then I think we need to talk to Yusof. He may know what this is all about because we don't. Perhaps we can try to rescue the bears but we shall need to plan."

Thanking Beminyak for his help, the boys made their way back to Professor Profundo and the girls. Tunku accompanied them. They did not know it but Berminyak was following them again. This was all getting very interesting and he wanted to know everything.

The Professor was relieved to see the boys. There was lots of hand-shaking and hugging all round although he hid his anxiety from the girls, he had been getting anxious about them, and he was thrilled to see Tunku again. Very soon however, Tunku left them. He had to find Matahari and particularly Hitam Malam and his tribe. The children and the Professor agreed that the best thing to do would be to return to the Kampong now that they knew where the bear cubs were and what was happening there. They would speak to Yusof and draw up an action plan. They broke camp and set off immediately. For once it was not raining and they maintained a reasonably good pace.

As soon as he saw Yusof, Professor Profundo called cheerily, "Yusof, My dear fellow, you will not guess what I have found in the forest – a clump of Nepenthes Rajah! Is that not wonderful? To date, they have only been found in Sarawak. This is history in the making! The girls helped me. Look! I brought a root with me. See how strong it is."

The Professor's enthusiasm was infectious. Engrossed in his botanical find, he had completely forgotten the plight of the poor bears.

The children on the other hand, could not wait to tell their tale. Yusof and Aishah were happy to see them all back safe and sound but as the children recited their story, Yusof looked more and more grim.

"Bapa, why are they hurting the bears?" Faradilla asked, the baby monkey still clinging to her.

"It is bile farming, Faradilla. They milk bile from the stomach of each bear. They only get a tiny drop of bile each day but it causes the bears terrible pain. They do it in unhygienic circumstances; the bears are never anaesthetised, they never receive veterinary care. And they are kept in those cages all their lives until they die. Fortunately some of them die early from infections and so on. At least then they are released from the torture, for it is indeed torture that is inflicted on them."

"But why? What do they do with the bile?"

"That is the point. It is used in Chinese medicine. They believe that bear bile cures all sorts of ills. Science does recognise that bear bile can cure several ailments but it is already synthesised in laboratories replicating the bile acid UDCA, using bile from slaughter house by-products and sold all around the world. Anything bear bile is claimed to cure can be cured by modern medicines and products from plants, for instance. I am told some airlines are even giving free bottles of it to their passengers as a promotional gimmick. That is particularly disgusting."

"Why do the Chinese not use modern medicines? I am Chinese. Mummee and Daddee only use modern medicines," Xin-Hui said.

"Yes, Xin-Hui, many Chinese people use modern medicines but some cling to their traditional remedies. Bile farming has been banned in Malagiar for several years now but it is very lucrative and it is not difficult to hide a bile farm away in the forest or in the middle of a palm oil plantation. A lot of these villagers who run bile farms are very, very poor and it provides an incredible source of income for them. They can make more money than they had ever dreamed of."

"We must rescue ALL the bears, not just the cubs," Joseph pointed out.

"That will not be easy. Even if you do rescue them, the adult bears have been in cages for years. Many of them will not be able to walk, their leg muscles will have wasted away. They would have to learn to walk again. They will all have infections in their tummies because of the holes there and they will all have to be operated on to have the holes repaired and those with tubes will have to have them removed. Most of them will also have to have their gall bladders removed because they will have become badly infected. They will be in tremendous pain; every movement will be agony for them. And how do you propose to move them?"

Bapa!" Ibrahim and Faradilla chorused simultaneously. "You must do it. You can. We know you can. You can get your friend, the veterinary man, to operate on them."

"We cannot leave them there, Yusof." Joseph was adamant.

Yusof sighed. "It will take a lot of work to prepare the centre to receive them. How many bears are there?"

Nobody knew.

"Very well. We must just do the best we can. The villagers will help I am sure and I shall have to contact my veterinary friends. We shall need their help. We shall have to transport the bears here somehow. I shall speak to the Headman of the Orang Asli. We shall need his expertise.

"The cubs can go back to their mothers in the forest," Ibrahim said. "Hitam Malam will be able to see to that."

"That would help but I shall have to check their health first. You never know what infections they may have picked up in that horrible place and we cannot risk them passing infections on to the other creatures of the forest."

The children spoke, all at once, "We shall have to organise transport for the bears if they cannot walk."

"How are we going to get in there?"

"How will we get the bears out of the cages?"

"Vinod, are you sure that Fat Superintendent woman carries the keys on her belt all the time?"

"Well, she did all the time I was there," Vinod replied. "We shall have to get the keys."

"How are we going to do that?"

"I don't know. We shall have to move very soon, perhaps in three or four days' time. I think we should all sleep on it and come up with a plan tomorrow." Joseph was tired and he could not think properly when he was tired.

"This whole exercise has to be carefully planned. Those bears are in a very bad state. How are you going to get them through the forest, all the way back here? This must all be thought through very carefully." Yusof, of course, was right.

The following day Yusof set off to find his old friend, the Head man of the Orang Asli. He had already spoken to several of the villagers who were now at work building big airy cages and an enclosure for the new bear arrivals. After he had spoken to the Head Man Yusof intended to call on his other friend, the veterinary surgeon.

The children and Professor Profundo had joined the villagers in building the new enclosure. It was hard work, but they never faltered. This was urgent!

When they stopped for lunch the children sat in a circle, trying to form a plan of action. "We shall have to get in there, open the gates, open the sheds, and then open all the cages.

That's the biggest problem. We know the fat Superintendent caries the keys. But how can we get them off her?"

"The keys are on a big metal ring," Vinod remembered. "If we could get that ring off her, we could get all the keys and simply unlock the doors."

"What about the Fat Superintendent, lah? Is she dangerous? What is she like? What about the bad men? How many of them are there?" Xin-Hui was anxious.

Vinod thought for a while. "The fat Superintendent is fat and ugly. Her clothes are too tight and she has bandy legs. She has black curly hair and it is very untidy. I do not think she would be able to move very quickly," he laughed. "And I saw only two men."

"But the monkey says there are four of them," Faradilla chipped in. "Do they live there?"

"I do not think so. There were a few huts around the compound but they seemed to be for storing food and that stuff, bile, and one was a sort of office. It was all very dirty and smelly." Vinod pulled a face as he remembered.

"If they do not live there the obvious thing to do will be to go in at night and rescue the bears while nobody is about," Toby suggested, pleased with himself.

"How would we get the keys?" Joseph was thinking hard."If there were four men, we need to know where the other two are. We need to know the Fat Superintendent's movements. Ibrahim, could one of the creatures watch her for us, just for a couple of days? She would not suspect a monkey. In fact, she would think it quite normal for a monkey to be about."

"If we can persuade one to leave the forest, it might work. But the creatures do not like to go out of the forest. It is a good idea. We can try,." said Ibrahim nodding in assent.

Joseph, as usual, was working out the best way to do things. "If we can get the bears out, we shall need help getting them back to the kampong. We cannot do that on our own. It is about ten kilometres directly through the forest. Perhaps we should go and find Tunku or Matahari this afternoon, see if they can help."

"They are very sick and in great pain. There is no path all the way which is wide

enough so we shall have to widen the paths."
Vinod sometimes surprised himself with his
reasoning.

"That is true."

"Why don't we ask for help, like last time,
when we built the fire break?" Toby said. "That
worked, and people even enjoyed themselves."

"But we do not have enough time."

"We can do it – if everyone joins in. Perhaps
the creatures would help as well." Toby was
beginning to enjoy this. At last he could see
a way forward.

"We shall have to speak to the monks, and
the priest, and the Imam, and the Granthi
again." "I am not afraid to speak to the monks
any more; they are kind," Xin-Hui said. "So I
can go to the temple on my own and you can
go to the church, Joseph, and Ibrahim can go
to the Imam and Vinod can go to the Granthi.
That will save us a lot of time."

The others agreed and set off immediately
to round up the help they needed.

Two hours later the children, elated, met
up again. The priest, the monks, the Imam
and the Granthi had all agreed to help them
widen the paths through the forest so that
the sick bears could be carried through.
However, they thought they would be working

on another firebreak. They did not know it was to transport sick bears - the children had omitted that detail.

Next, Ibrahim decided to go into the forest and find Tunku. He would ask the creatures if they would also help to widen those paths.

"We are coming too," chorused the other children. "Well, not the girls," Ibrahim said.

"We are coming too," said Faradilla boldly. "Besides, I need to find this baby's Mummy." "Faradilla is right," said Xin-Hui, determinedly.

Faradilla was trying to loosen the baby monkey's fingers, which were grasping her long black hair very tightly and it did not want to let go.

Ibrahim gave in. He was no match for the girls when they were determined.

No sooner had the children entered the forest than "Sshhh!" Ibrahim cautioned them. "Listen! We can hear all the creatures now. This part of the forest is alive."

The children agreed Ibrahim was right. A cheeky gibbon was already peering down at them through the branches, and there was a lot of scuffling in the undergrowth.

Berminyak had been loitering on the outskirts of the kampong, not quite brave enough to leave the forest with so many humans and dogs about but there were a lot of chickens there, which tempted him. He could smell them through his flickering tongue. And then there was that small monkey the girl was carrying about. That would make a tasty snack. Perhaps he would follow the children. He could return to the kampong later.

Word of the children's presence spread quickly through the forest and soon enough there was Number One Son swinging towards them. Ibrahim told Number One Son they needed help.

"Tunku, my father, has already organised it. Everyone is ready. We wait for you. AND I am even postponing my Naming Day so that we can help you."

"Oh, Number One Son, I am very, very grateful," Ibrahim said."We also need to find this baby's Mummy." He pointed at the little monkey clinging to Faradilla. "They became separated in the dead part of the forest and the baby got lost."

"I shall pass on the word. And when the bears are rescued, I shall have my Naming Day." Ibrahim felt very guilty. "Oh, Number One Son, I am so sorry we have delayed it."

"I do not understand how you can talk so easily to the creatures and we cannot." Vinod was a little jealous of Ibrahim's ability. He desperately wanted to talk to the animals as well. But he knew he never would.

"Now all we have to do is get the parents to join us. So, we have to speak to them tonight." "Ah, I know Mummee and Daddee will help," said Xin-Hui. "They feel better if they are with me."

"My parents will be no trouble. They believe I am setting my little brother a good example," Vinod responded.

"Mine are pretty laid back really. And they like being involved," Joseph shrugged. "They'll be OK."

CHAPTER 7

Yusof, Aishah and Profesor Profundo were sitting on the anjung, taking tea and cakes when the children returned. It was a peaceful part of the day. Professor Profundo was still chattering enthusiastically about the Nepenthes Rajah he had found. "Do you realize that it is the largest pitcher plant in the world?"

"That is a very wild and untamed part of the forest, Professor. I am not surprised you have found it there, and indeed, there may be several more species there which we do not know about." Yusof was laughing fondly at his friend.

"Oh, My Dear Boy!" exclaimed the Professor who was so excited he could hardly contain himself. He was hot and sticky. Taking off his panama, he mopped his brow. "Well. That is it! We really have to go back." He stood up and paced up and down.

Yusof and Aishah could not help being affected by the Professor's enthusiasm. "I am sure we can arrange that, Professor."

"Ah, children," Yusof called as the children trudged towards the house, "I have good news for you."

"What is it, Bapa?"

"The Headman and his people are building stretchers for the bears right now and they will liaise with the creatures so that we can get them to the kampong. He said you are to meet him in the glade tonight."

"Oh, Bapa!" Faradilla threw her arms around him. "I knew you could do it." "He wants to meet us all?" Xin-Hui and Vinod asked.

"We can go to the glade? All of us?" Faradilla queried.

"I think you girls are too young" Joseph felt very protective towards the girls.

"No we are not. We fought in the great fight just as well as anybody else." "They are right." spoke up Ibrahim. "They should be allowed to come too."

"Oh, alright, if Yusof and Aishah agree, but we still have to get the bears out," said Joseph, worried.

Ibrahim told Yusof that they had already enlisted help from both the humans and the creatures in widening the forest paths. Yusof laughed. "I should have realized that you children cannot be stopped once you make up your minds."

Unexpectedly, Tunku arrived. The children were delighted to see him, as were Yusof, Aishah and Professor Profundo. Arm draped carelessly round Ibrahim's shoulders, as was his wont, Tunku tapped Ibrahim's arm. Ibrahim listened as Tunku spoke to him. Then he nodded in approval. "That's the best idea ever, Tunku."

Katak, gambolling with the other village dogs, started barking fiercely on the edge of the kampong. Berminyak hissed angrily at him. He would have had that chicken, were it not for the dratted dog. Katak stood his ground and Berminyak had no choice but to turn and slither back into the forest undergrowth. The village dogs all rushed up, barking in frenzy, and all Berminyak could do was writhe in disgust in the undergrowth.

The children, momentarily distracted by Katak, resumed their debate.

"Tunku has a good idea" Ibrahim said. "He will send in a whole troop of macaques to the compound. They will climb about the place and will be able to get in and out of buildings. They will find out all we need to know."

"Oh, Tunku, that's a great idea! Of course, monkeys get everywhere so they won't be considered unusual," Joseph said.

"But that horrible place is on the far side of the forest. When we rescue the bears, it will take us too long to get there and then we shall have to sleep in the forest again. And it's monsoon time, lah." Xin-Hui shuddered. She was quite sure that she did not like camping out in the forest. There were too many creepy-crawlies; she was already badly bitten; and there were far too many leeches.

"I have been thinking about that, Xin-Hui. There is a road there so we can get there by road. I think I should telephone Shirley Pooper. She always wants another 'scoop', and perhaps she can take us in that old jeep of hers," responded Joseph.

"Oh, yes!" The children liked that idea.

Initially, when they first met, they had not liked Shirley Pooper. She was a pretty zany woman. But as time progressed and she began to understand what they were doing, she wrote some very good articles in the South East Asia Gazette about the children and the forest. Her boss had been so pleased with her articles that he had given Shirley a pay rise. And her photographer, Bert, had got a pay rise as well. So now she was very inclined to help the children.

Shirley Pooper was in her office at the South East Asia Gazette. She had a nice office all to herself now and she was the principle journalist on the paper. How times change! She thought back to stories she had written which had changed her from a poorly paid junior journalist under constant threat of being sacked. She thought fondly of 'those Doughty Warriors' as she had dubbed the children. *'What are they going to get up to this holiday?* she wondered. *Perhaps I had better give them a call.'* Bert, the photographer, was happy too. His photographs of the forest, the children, the villagers and the creatures had sold all over the world and he had achieved a not inconsiderable degree of fame. In fact, he was soon to put on a big exhibition of his photographs. If the exhibition was successful, he would take it all over the world.

Shirley's boss, Sam, the Editor, poked his head round the door. "What's the latest hot stuff, Shirley? What have you got for me?"

"Not much, Sam. A story about that guy who got murdered on his boat by pirates but that's it right now."

"Well, I'm sure you can make something out of that." Sam smiled at her indulgently.

'How times have changed, Sam,' Shirley smiled to herself. *'Only a few months ago you were threatening every five minutes to fire me, and you paid me peanuts.'*

"O.K., Sam. It's nearly ready. Give me an hour."

Just then Shirley's 'phone rang. She picked it up. "Hello, young Joseph. I was just thinking about you. How are things? What are you children up to these days?"

Shirley listened intently as Joseph spoke. *'Aha! These children are great.'* she thought.

'Another story! Another scoop! Bert will be glad too. Yes!! She punched the air with her fist. "We shall need you to take us in your car, Shirley."

"When do you want to do this, Joseph? Where do you want us to go?"

"Soon! We're waiting for the feedback from the macaques. They've gone to the bile farm and are gathering information for us. They should be able to let Tunku know tonight. I'll 'phone you again as soon as we've got news."

Shirley rushed out of her office, slamming the door behind her. She was looking for Bert. "Bert! Bert! We need to talk."

Joseph switched off his 'phone feeling mildly triumphant. Shirley was on side and would bring Bert with her.

The fat superintendent.

CHAPTER 8

So engrossed was she in what she was doing that she failed to notice the small macaque The Fat Superintendent was sitting at a rickety old makeshift desk in one of the sheds inside the compound. The shed, or office as she liked to call it, was filthy and the desk was covered in greasy grime and dust which came from years of neglect and filth. Cobwebs and spiders were plentiful there and many, many insects were caught in those cobwebs which had never been removed. The chair she sat on wobbled precariously under her great weight. With difficulty she pulled herself out of the chair and bending down, huffing and puffing, she placed a folded piece of cardboard under one of the chair legs. She picked up the large bag at her feet and rummaged inside it. Then sitting down again with a big sigh, she pulled out a container full of hot noodles in greasy chicken soup and a pair of chopsticks. She lifted the container to her mouth and using the chopsticks, began slurping the noodles noisily in to her mouth. Grease dribbled down her three chins. She made no effort to remove it.

When she had finished the noodles and soup she put down the container and rummaged in the large bag again. She pulled out a paper bag stuffed full of doughnuts: a chocolate doughnut, a vanilla doughnut, and a jam doughnut and immediately started cramming the chocolate doughnut into her mouth – as much as she could, as fast as she could. She munched her way happily through all three doughnuts. Then wiping her mouth with the back of her hand, and wiping her greasy, sticky hand on her shirt, she belched loudly, a long, rumbling belch and then another. She sat back and sticking her short fat legs out in front of her, she stretched, throwing her arms up over her head into the air, revealing black, hairy armpits enfolded in the sagging flesh of her arms. She dropped the paper bags and container on the floor and left them there, along with other rotting, stinking debris from previous meals.

On the desk in front of her was a stained and grubby ledger. She pulled it towards her and, wrapping her short, pudgy fingers round a stubby pencil, she started to write, adding up, subtracting, sucking and licking her sticky fingers which still tasted of chocolate and vanilla, as she wrote. She spotted a dollop of jam on the ledger and tried to lick it off but it merely smudged.

Sitting still and quiet on top of the perimeter fence, watching intently with unblinking gaze her every move was a small macaque.

Finally she put the pencil down and smiled contentedly. The Baron would be pleased. The figures added up and a big profit had been made. She lifted a finger to her nose. The nail was long and dirty, black with grime. She stuck it up her nostril and wiggled it about. She unpacked the contents of her nostril and wiped it off on the underside of the desk. Tonight she would have a shower and wash her hair and tomorrow she would put on her prettiest shirt, because the Baron would be coming for his weekly inspection. She lifted her arm and lazily tugged at a large spider's web suspended from the beam of the shed. As she tugged, the resident spider, which happened to be very large, black and hairy, rushed towards her outstretched fingers. Yelping, the Fat Superintendent withdrew her fingers, but the sticky spider's web clung to them. She shook her hand; the web stubbornly stuck. Frustrated, she tried to remove the web with her other hand but then both hands were covered in it. She repeatedly wiped her hands against her trousers until the whole web was removed. She had better find Ah Kong.

She waddled out of the shed across the compound, calling Ah Kong. The small macaque on the fence could hear her thighs swish, swishing against each other as she went.

Eventually she found Ah Kong, fast asleep, curled up in a ball in the shade at the edge of the compound. She kicked him. She kicked him again and again until he stirred. He woke up and swore at her, pulling himself up to a sitting position and then standing up. Neither of them was aware of the monkey watching from the shadows.

"Where are the others?" she asked him. "They will have to tidy this place up. The Baron is coming tomorrow. And that bear, Kulat – you will have to move his cage outside. He is not yielding any more bile. Leave him out there - let him starve to death. Oh, and be sure to cut off his paws just before he dies. They do not have any value, remember, if he dies before they are cut off."

Ah Kong grinned. He did not much like the Fat Superintendent, but he was well paid as long as he kept his mouth shut and asked no questions. He told the Fat Superintendent that two of the men had gone into the forest to see if the bear traps had worked and the other had taken the lorry with the bile to market. They would all be back in time for the next bile milking session, so she was not to worry.

Sure enough, within the hour, all four men were back in the compound. They made their way to the first bear shed. As soon as the door opened, the bears inside, who had been relatively quiet, began to wail and shriek in earnest. They were terrified of these men, who over and over again, caused them so much pain. They milked all the bears except Kulat, whose cage they picked up and dumped unceremoniously outside.

Kulat had been cooped up in the dingy bear shed for so long that the bright light outside blinded him. He could see nothing. As his cage crashed to the ground, every bone in his body shook. He lay for a long while, winded and in pain, unable to see, wondering what was happening to him. Then it started to rain. At first, Kulat could not believe his luck. How long was it since he had last experienced rain? He could not remember. All his memory was contained within that fearful shed.

This rain was warm, refreshing and soothing, to his aching body. But it was monsoon rain, and soon Kulat was soaked through, right to his skin. He was an old, tired, and sick bear and he started to shiver violently. There was no shelter here from the rain. His cage was so small that he could not even sit up. Finally the rain stopped just as suddenly as it had started but Kulat was soaked through. The little macaque stole a biscuit from the Fat Superintendent's desk, and brought it to Kulat who took it gratefully. He licked the rain off his paws. He had heard what they did to bears when they were old and sick. There would be no food for him now, no water. He had been left to rot and die.

It was dusk. The Fat Superintendent and the four bad men set off for home. They locked the compound gates as they left, travelling together in a rickety old truck. The small macaque headed back to the forest to tell Tunku what he had seen.

The following day, the Fat Superintendent and the four bad men arrived a little earlier than usual at the bear bile farm. She was wearing a very tight bright orange top, shiny like Lycra, and low cut so that her large bosoms exploded over the top like ripe melons. She wore a new white skirt which was far too short. Her bottom was so large that the skirt hemline rose up at the back and her wobbly, fleshy thighs could be seen swish swishing together as she tottered along on ridiculously high heels. She had washed and crimped her hair, applied kohl and mascara to her eyes and smeared her mouth with bright red lipstick. The Baron was coming! She had heard the rumours that his wife had left him and, she, the Fat Supervisor, was hopelessly in love with the Baron. She would make sure he noticed her. She would make herself so indispensible to him that he would not be able to manage without her and eventually, he would fall in love with her and marry her.

This was the Fat Superintendent's plan and nothing would deter her. She had started by making this bile farm profitable. She faithfully reported everything that anyone said, or even thought, to the Baron in the belief that her tale-telling would prove her loyalty to him.

Her tittle-tattle had already caused Ah Kong a great deal of trouble when one evening, a little inebriated, he had expressed his real opinion of the Baron. His relationship with the Baron had never been the same since and unbeknown to her, he held a grudge against the Fat Superintendent, but he bided his time.

The Baron's shiny new car rolled in to the compound. Nobody had noticed the arrival of a small troop of monkeys. The monkeys made themselves scarce; it was not in their interest to be noticed. The Fat Superintendent waddled happily towards the Baron's car. He opened the door and climbed out. As he did so she stood, leaning forward, arms outstretched, bosoms heaving, eyelids fluttering, cheek extended for a kiss. But the Baron ignored her and strode past making for the office. She turned and waddled after him as quickly as she could but she had to lean forward to keep her balance on those high heels, which made her skirt ride up even higher at the back. Ah Kong, behind her, averted his eyes. What a horrible sight!

The Baron made straight for the office. All he was interested in was the ledger. *'Ah, there it is!'* He ran his finger down the columns of figures.

"Yes!" The figures were good. The Fat Superintendent was doing a good job. He made no attempt to see the bears or to discuss them. He turned and headed back to the car.

The Fat Superintendent was determined that he should notice her. "Baron! Baron!" Bowing, smirking, ingratiating, and subservient "Let me give you a tour of the bear sheds. I am sure you would like to see them," she suggested.

"No. I would not."

Ah Kong almost felt sorry for the Fat Supervisor.

The Baron was thinking of the nice little girl he had met the previous evening and whom he was about to take out to lunch today. She was young and pretty. Having lunch with her would cheer him up. Ever since that horrible Prime Minister had sent him to prison and confiscated his palm oil plantations, his life had not been very happy. His wife had left him (all she had been interested in was his money) and he was having to rebuild his life. Thanks to the bile farms he was establishing around Malagiar, he was beginning to do very well again.

He made for his car, only to shriek in anger. A pair of monkeys had wrenched off a wind screen wiper, and one of his wing mirrors.

They were sitting on top of the car, admiring themselves in the mirror they had stolen. His lovely, shiny new car! The baron shouted in rage, waving his arms. The monkeys scampered off, taking the wing mirror with them. He examined the car carefully. A monkey had clearly got inside, and defecated on the driver's seat.

"Ugh!" He shouted at the Fat Superintendent to clean it up.

"Yes, Baron." She waddled up with a dirty old rag. *'Oh, My Darling, I would do anything for you, even this! One day you will realise you cannot manage without me. I shall run your whole life for you. Your every word will be my command, and, in return, you will love me. How you will love me!'* She thought as she dabbed ineffectively at the mess.

The Baron pushed her roughly aside and rubbed the mess off with a cloth he found inside the car. Once the seat was cleaned he climbed in, slamming the door behind him and drove off without so much as another glance at the Fat Superintendent. She stood forlornly in the middle of the compound, watching the car disappear down the road.

Meanwhile, the Macaques were infiltrating every nook, cranny and crevice they could.

Silently they scampered along the perimeter fence and crouched in the shadows. They explored and made a mental note of what they found. At the back of the compound, one enterprising little fellow was digging his way underneath one of the bear sheds. The sheds did not have solid floors and he eventually got in. Chattering very quietly, he spoke to the caged bears. They could not believe their ears or their eyes; perhaps something WAS going to happen for the better.

They had seen Berminyak of course but most of them thought it had been a dream, a mirage. They had been incarcerated in this shed for countless years and no creature other than the Fat Superintendent and her four henchmen had ever previously entered here. The small macaque told them he would return and quickly took his leave. There was a lot more work to do. He crept over to the next shed and dug his way into that as well.

In this shed, the bears had not been visited by Berminyak.

"Who are you and what do you here?" rumbled one of the bears.

"Forgive me, great bear, but I have been sent to find out what is happening here in these sheds."

"Who sent you?" rumbled the bear.

"Tunku, Lord of the Canopies, sent me. He sent me on behalf of Hitam Malam, the great bear of the forest."

"Hitam Malam," the bears repeated the name in a sighing whisper. "Hitam Malam!"

"From memories of long ago, I remember Hitam Malam. I am Abu. He may recall my name of old."

"I must go. I must report back but I shall return. And so will many others. That is my solemn promise." And so the little monkey left them.

The bears were confused, trying to remember their distant past when they too were free to roam the forest at will.

"Can you remember grass?"

"Do you remember what it was like to lie down in a dry bracken nest?"

"Do you remember the moon shining bright?"

"I remember."

"I DO remember."

"Yes, I remember. Aah, the fresh green smell of it."

The bears settled down in their cages, remembering distant memories, dreaming of the past.

CHAPTER 9

The children were creeping through the damp, soggy forest heading for the glade. It was very dark and wet and Faradilla and Xin-Hui held hands, whispering encouragement to each other. Vinod, trying hard to be brave, managed to keep up with Ibrahim and Joseph. Toby held back, keeping an eye out for the girls. He did not want them to get left behind.

"You know, Ibrahim, if it keeps on raining like this, we don't have a chance of getting the bears back to the kampong. It's just too slippery and wet."

"The monsoon season is supposed to be over. It is just a little late this year." Ibrahim answered. "We shall just have to pray to Allah for dry weather."

"Well, I shall pray to my God and you can pray to Mohammad."

"Joseph, Mohammad is not a god, he is a Prophet! Allah is god." Ibrahim was shocked. "Sorry Ibrahim. I know that; I just forgot."

"It is not raining now. We just have to hope and pray that it will not do so when we rescue the bears."

The children all carried torches and by now Ibrahim knew the route well; nonetheless, it took them half an hour to reach the glade. The three older boys were reasonably confident but Vinod, Xin-Hui and Faradilla huddled close together. Vinod and Xin-Hui jumped at every sound. Joseph and Ibrahim of course had visited the glade before. Nothing could have prepared the other children for what they were about to see.

When they emerged into the vast cathedral-like space Toby, Vinod and the girls gasped in amazement. It was a magnificent hall, lit by tiny fireflies. The trees were intricately carved columns and pillars and the branches overhead formed a rich and delicately carved dome. It was beautiful, this special and secret meeting place of the creatures. They were sworn to secrecy. They would never, never tell where it was. Tunku and Hitam Malam were already there, waiting. Without warning and without a sound the headman of the Orang

Asli was suddenly in front of them. He carried a spear, and looked particularly fierce in the moonlight. Xin-Hui stopped in her tracks and squeezed Faradilla's hand very hard. "Ow!" whispered Faradilla "You are hurting me."

"Sorry. He is so scary, lah!"

A soft rumbling advertised Matahari's approach. He was followed by Cahaya Bulan and their new baby son, Guruh.

"Oohh, he is lovely. So sweet!" Faradilla and Xin-Hui were entranced by the baby elephant. Cahaya Bulan stood protectively over her son but she allowed the girls to go up to him, cuddle him and stroke him. Playfully he head butted Xin-Hui. She squealed in delight.

A troop of macaques arrived, unusually quiet for them. This was the troop Tunku had sent into the compound. The head of the troop, sitting on the ground in front of the others, reported all that they had seen.

"There were about twenty bear cubs in cages stacked up outside the sheds. They had a little shelter, but not much. They say that once they are three years' old, they will be taken into the sheds. They do not yet know what for. But we saw! We saw what they are doing there. It is terrible, terrible!"

Overwhelmed by what he was telling, the monkey dropped his head and sat for a few seconds in silence. Then he continued "There are two sheds, about twenty bears in each. They are packed from floor to ceiling in tiny, cramped cages. They do not have room to sit up or stand. They do not have solid floors to lie on but round bars. The cages are made of metal and are padlocked. The Fat Superintendent and the bad men leave the compound every evening at dusk." The monkey paused for breath.

Hitam Malam rolled his head and drummed his paws on the ground in distress. He hated to hear this but he had to if he was going to do anything about it.

"The bears have been there for a long time. They have little memory of the forest but, Hitam Malam, one bear, Abu, thinks you may remember him."

Hitam Malam searched his memory, and then it came back to him.

"Why, we were playmates when we were young. He was not much more than a cub and then he disappeared and was never seen again."

"Now you know where he went," Tunku said grimly.

Ibrahim was thinking hard. "We shall have to do this at night. Even if we get into the compound and get the sheds open, we still cannot open the cages."

"How are we going to see our way through the forest at night?" Toby asked. "Leave that to us," the head man said.

The monkey intervened. "That Fat Superintendent is frightened of monkeys. She hates us.

We have a plan. If we, the whole troop, fly at her together, I think we can bring her down and then while she is on the ground, fending us off, one of us can steal the keys from her. She will not know what we have done. We shall act just as she is about to leave the compound in the evening. Hopefully she will be so anxious to get away that she will not notice we have taken her keys," he finished smugly.

The whole troop of monkeys behind him chittered and chattered in delight, waving their little hands in the air at the prospect of such an adventure.

"It might just work," Joseph said slowly.

"It is the best idea so far," Ibrahim chipped in.

"Then, we must start work on widening the paths tomorrow. If we all work together, as we did building the fire break, we should finish within a couple of days. We only have to widen it enough to get through this time and then it can grow back again." Joseph was feeling more confident. The head man and Tunku nodded in agreement and Matahari rumbled.

"Do not worry, Hitam Malam, we shall rescue all your bears, I promise," Faradilla said kindly, stroking the great bear who was beside himself with grief.

So they all agreed. The paths would be widened, then the headman of the Orang-Asli, Matahari, Tunku and Hitam Malam would organise the transportation of the bears back to the kampong once the children had got them out of the compound. But the children had to get them out.

"Oh," the monkey added. "There is something else. One of the men there is Ah Kong. We believe it is the same Ah Kong who worked for the evil palm oil baron when they were trying to fire the forest."

"Ah Kong?" "Ah Kong!" "Ahh."

"And," said the monkey "a man in a shiny black car turned up to day. We believe he was The Fat Superintendent's boss. Both she and

Ah Kong were kow-towing to him." Who can that be?" they all wondered.

"We shall have to wait to find out. Let's get the bears out first," Joseph said.

The Orang-Asli had made stretchers and containers for the bears, although not enough. Now they knew there were forty adult bears and twenty cubs, they would have to make more but they could cope with that in a day. They and the creatures would be ready to transport the bears in two days' time, once the paths had been widened.

"What about Bapa? Has he got enough room for all those bears?" Faradilla asked hesitantly. "Bapa will not turn any bear away. He will find room somehow," Ibrahim answered her confidently although he, too, was a little worried now that he knew there were so many bears.

The children took their leave of the head man and the creatures and made their way home. On the way, they chatted:

"We'll have to have a lie-in tomorrow, otherwise we shall be too tired." "What about the parents if we are out all night again?"

"We shall have to say we are exploring with Professor Profundo." "But that is telling lies."

"Tell them the truth if you like." They walked on in silence.

"If the Professor comes with us, it would be a half-truth," said Vinod hopefully. "That is better than a whole lie."

Finally Joseph said "I think we have to tell the parents the truth but just do not let them think it is dangerous. Simply say we are going to rescue some bears with the help of the Orang- Asli and the creatures. That should be alright. What about your parents, Xin-Hui? They are the most fearful."

"I think that would work, particularly if I tell Mummee Cahaya Bulan will be with us." Xin- Hui was keeping her fingers tightly crossed.

They found Yusof working hard with some of the villagers, building new compounds for the bears.

"Bapa, the monkeys think there are forty adult bears and twenty cubs." Ibrahim told his father.

"Sixty bears! Goodness gracious! That is a lot of bears." Yusof exclaimed.

By time the children surfaced the following day, Yusof and some of the villagers were already hard at work, building dens and compounds for the new arrivals. There were a lot to build – so many bears! Many people, including some of the villagers, Orang Asli, Buddhist monks, Sikhs, Moslem clerics and Christian priests were already at work widening the forest paths. Based on previous experience, they had had the good sense to bring cutting tools, thick gloves, boots, secateurs, spades and forks.

Most of them had worked previously with the children when building the fire break but they were still a little wary of the creatures. Matahari was there with Ribut, Halilintar and Bijaksana. Hantu joined Hitam Malam. The bears worked with particular intensity and haste. Mr and Mrs Brown were there, Mr and Mrs Singh and of course, Mr and Mrs Chan. Yusof was there, and Professor Profundo. Mrs Chan was disappointed not to see Cahaya Bulan. She had been looking forward to meeting her favourite elephant again.

Shirley Pooper and Bert arrived to take photographs. Joseph had already briefed Shirley on the telephone, and she and Bert were sworn to secrecy until after the rescue.

Humans, apes and monkeys hacked and pulled at the undergrowth. The elephants bulldozed the larger, harder bushes and trees. Pangolins, lizards and civet cats smoothed the paths as best they could so as to give the bears a less bumpy ride.

They worked on until it was dusk and they could no longer see properly. As the humans turned for home, Mrs Chan could not believe her eyes. There waiting for her was Cahaya Bulan and she had a tiny beautiful calf with her.

"Oohh! Oohh! My very own Moonlight. How are you? And you have a baby. How wonderful." Mrs Chan felt she had a particular relationship with Cahaya Bulan. Without hesitating, she went up to her and hugged her trunk. She stroked the baby. "I had so hoped to see you again and now you have a baby too. I am so very happy." Mrs Chan smiled ecstatically. Cahaya Bulan wrapped her trunk gently around Mrs Chan. She would remember this moment for the rest of her life.

Aishah as always had prepared a wonderful feast for everyone on the padang. The village women had hung candles and lanterns round the perimeter and it was very pretty. Food was laid out on tables all round and the children sat down happily, surrounded by friends.

"We have made such good progress that we should finish tomorrow," the head man of the Orang Asli told Yusof. "But I do not think the children should go to the bear bile farm tomorrow night. They should rest, and then go the following evening."

This was sage advice so Yusof agreed. Calling Ibrahim and Joseph to come over to him, he told them what the head man had advised. Although they were impatient to rescue the bears, they agreed that it was sensible advice and would give them a chance to catch up on some much needed sleep. Joseph and Ibrahim rushed off to tell the others.

The villagers and helpers did not know why they were widening the paths through the forest. They thought it was simply another firebreak. The children had decided that nobody should know the truth in case any of them knew the Fat Superintendent or any of her henchmen and inadvertently told them what was happening. Shirley Pooper and Bert had also been sworn to secrecy.

The following day everyone worked hard again. The creatures and the Orang Asli never stopped. But they all knew that it WAS the last day and that they were nearing the end of their task, which gave them encouragement. And then they broke through to the edge of the forest. There in front of them was the road leading to the bear compound. Apart from that, all that could be seen was the palm oil plantation, miles and miles of it.

Joseph and Ibrahim did not want the villagers and other humans to know there was a road there so they asked the elephants to line up along the edge of the forest and block the view. Nobody would try to get past **them.**

When people realised that they could go no further they turned back, realizing their task was completed. Yusof, Professor Profundo and the children ran up and down the lines of returning workers, thanking them for what they had done. There was to be a special feast on the padang tonight and Yusof was to make an announcement, so they were asked to please stay.

CHAPTER 10

The creatures had departed. Everyone was impressed by how hard they had worked and how uncomplaining they were. It was a marvel that wild creatures should co-operate so closely with humans! Back at the kampong they made their way to the padang, washed and sat down to eat the candle and lantern-lit feast spread out before them which Aishah and other village women had so painstakingly prepared.

The children were elated and a little fearful. Tomorrow night they would be rescuing the bears! The paths back to the kampong were clear. They just prayed that nothing would go wrong. Sensing her mood, Katak snuggled up to Faradilla.

Standing on the anjung Yusof banged on a dustbin lid to get everyone's attention. They stopped talking and turned towards him.

"Ladies and gentlemen, firstly I wish to thank you all for your efforts over these past two days. You and the creatures have helped us to clear the way. We shall be eternally grateful to you. We cannot tell you just yet why we need the firebreaks cleared but it is connected with what I am about to tell you.

As most of you know, we have started a charity here, at the kampong, together with Mr and Mrs Brown, Mr and Mrs Singh, and Mr and Mrs Chan, for the care of damaged wild creatures. With the help of these kind people we have raised enough money to support the Centre for the next six months. Extra revenue will be raised on an ongoing basis and through subscription and entry fees. The government has given us enough extra land and we are in the process of building more up-to-date sheds, nests, platforms, compounds and living areas for these creatures.

Our aim is to rehabilitate them wherever possible but sometimes the creatures which come to us are too badly wounded or damaged to return to the wild, in which case we intend to look after them for the rest of their lives. It is important that we live in harmony with nature and the more we understand of the creatures and their needs, the more able we shall be to do that. Just as we need our own space, so do they. We shall try very hard to ensure that at our Centre, the creatures get their own space. We shall open the Centre to the public . It will have a classroom where people can learn about the forest, its inhabitants and the rich plant life it supports. There will be a small cafe and a rest room and there will be walkways so that people can see the creatures without disturbing them. There will be plenty of areas where people can just sit and watch. But the spaces we provide will be primarily for the creatures.

We do not intend to protect the public from the creatures but to protect the creatures from the public.

Of course I shall continue with my work in the field of pharmacognosis. It is far too important to overlook. And Professor Profundo will be visiting us on a very regular basis to pursue his biological research. So, you see, this will be a preservation centre not just for the creatures but for the forest too.

I regret that we shall have to charge a small entry fee," he smiled ruefully "but it will all go towards the upkeep of the creatures in our care.

The Centre will be called **The Forest Sanctuary**, and will be opened officially by the Prime Minister of Malagiar on Thursday next week. You are all invited to attend and we hope," he added slyly, "to have some very special new guests by then."

The padang erupted. Everyone stood up, clapping and cheering. The children, who had not realized how soon the Centre would be opening, were especially thrilled. They clapped and cheered louder than anyone else. Professor Profundo tossed his panama into the air and gave Aishah the biggest, squeeziest hug he could. Faradilla and Xin-Hui were so excited that they just had to dance.

In the trees and undergrowth in the forest around them, the word was spread and they could hear the creatures also rejoicing.

Shirley Pooper was scribbling as fast as she could. She had taped Yusof's speech, and hoped she would be able to play it back in the peace and quiet of her own office. Bert was running around everywhere taking photographs. They would be attending the opening of the Forest Sanctuary of course but this preview would make good entertaining reading.

What a happy evening!

Despite their concerns about the following day, the children fell asleep very quickly that night. The next morning they got up late. After all, they would probably be out all night rescuing the bears. As she thought of what was to come that day, Xin-Hui shivered with excitement and some considerable fear. Perhaps she would go to the temple and light some joss sticks. She was not alone in her trepidation. Vinod quickly visited the Gurdwara and said a little prayer, Ibrahim visited the mosque with his father, Yusof and Patrick went to early morning mass at the Catholic church.

The children gathered on Yusof's anjung at lunch time. They spent the next hour or so going over their plan. They were to meet the Orang Asli and the creatures on the edge of the forest where they would be waiting. Then it was up to the children to get into the bear compound and release the bears from the cages. Bert and Shirley Pooper would go with them. The creatures and the Orang Asli would escort the bears through the forest to the Forest Sanctuary (how grand the name sounded) where Yusof would be waiting for them with two veterinary surgeons and some of the villagers who would help settle the bears down.

Shirley Pooper and Bert soon arrived, rattling along in her old jalopy. She knew she would never get Bert, his equipment, the Professor and six children in there so she had attached a trailer to the back and had thrown lots of cushions on the floor of the trailer. The children would be comfortable enough there. In case it rained she had put six umbrellas in the trailer as well. The Professor could sit in the front of the car and Bert and his equipment on the back seat. Professor Profundo was busily chatting to Bert about his Nementhes Rajah. He wanted Bert to come on his next exhibition and take photographs of the plant. Bert was actually quite interested.

It was time to go. Faradilla said good-bye to the baby monkey whose mother she had not yet found. It would be safer waiting on the anjung. The Professor, Bert and the children piled into Shirley Pooper's car and trailer and off they went, bumping along, on their way to the other side of the forest. It was fun sitting in the trailer and the rain held off. As they got closer to the bear compound the children stopped chattering and kept a careful lookout.

"I just hope we can get those bears out. What if we cannot get the cages open?" Vinod asked. "If the monkeys can get the keys, it will be fine. If not, we shall just have to do our best," Joseph answered.

"Don't worry, Vinod. We'll do it," said Toby, cheerful as always. "If we won the great fight, we can do just about anything."

Back at the kampong, Faradilla's adopted baby monkey was curled up on a cushion waiting for Faradilla to return. Some instinct made him turn his head. Immediately he jumped up, high in the air, shrieking, tiny teeth bared. Berminyak, head on the cushion, cleft tongue smelling the air, was furious. Foiled again! Aishah, hearing the commotion, emerged from the kitchen brandishing a broom. She shooed Berminyak away. Scooping up the baby monkey she took him into the house for his own safety. *'The sooner we find your Mummy, the better,'* she muttered.

CHAPTER 11

Arriving at the edge of the forest, Shirley parked the car in a covert, hidden from view, and the children clambered out. There was no movement, no sound coming from the forest. Warily they moved forward, Professor Profundo, Shirley Pooper and Bert keeping close by. They saw Matahari first then Ribut, Halilintar and Bijaksana. *'Those elephants are so impressive,'* thought Bert as he took some quick photographs of them. Hitam Malam was there with Hantu and Tunku with several members of his tribe, and many other apes and monkeys. And the Orang Asli were there. The elephants were wearing harnesses round their chests, to which the Orang Asli would attach the stretchers they were carrying, mounted on bamboo poles. Each elephant had a harness over its back as well, from which bamboo and rattan containers would hang. The children greeted the Orang Asli and the creatures with relief. It felt so much better knowing they were all there.

They waited until it was nearly dusk. Professor Profundo elected to wait in the forest with the Orang Asli and the creatures. Once the light had faded, the children padded quietly down the road accompanied by Shirley Pooper and Bert. Very nervous, senses heightened, they were aware of every sound around them. The Orang Asli and the creatures waited patiently.

There was a small copse near the entrance to the compound where the children, Shirley and Bert would hide until the Fat Superintendent and her henchmen had gone.

Inside the compound, there was a commotion. The Fat Superintendent was chasing a small monkey which had stolen her ledger. The monkey was waving the ledger over its head as, standing upright, it ran away from her.

"Ah Kong, Ah Kong!" she shouted, "Come and kill this horrid thing."

Ah Kong and the other three men were standing around laughing. None of them particularly liked the Fat Superintendent and she looked very funny tottering along after that monkey.

"Ah Kong!" she shrieked. " Get my ledgers. The Baron will punish you if you do not!"

Outside the compound the children heard the Fat Superintendent shrieking. They guessed it must be her. *'The Baron? Who is The Baron? Surely it can't be the evil palm oil Baron'.* Joseph was thinking fast. *'She certainly called Ah Kong. Can it possibly be the evil palm oil Baron and his foreman?'*

Inside the compound, confusion reigned. Ah Kong and the other three bad men joined the Fat Superintendent chasing the monkey with the ledger. The rest of the troop joined in the fray, dashing this way and that, screeching and tossing the ledger from one to another. They were having a great time but the Fat Superintendent had completely lost her temper and her head. She screamed at Ah Kong, she screamed at the other men, she screamed at the monkeys. Ah Kong brandished a rifle. He fired it but missed.

The children listened anxiously to all the commotion. "They've got guns." Toby whispered.

'I hope they do not kill any of those brave monkeys."

'No, they will not be able to. The monkeys are too quick for them." "It is alright. They will be gone before we go in," Ibrahim said.

One of the monkeys dropped the ledger on the ground a few feet in front of the Fat Superintendent, before scampering off. She tottered forward, breathing heavily, and bent down with difficulty to retrieve it. Her cheeks were red from the exertion and her hair was dishevelled. Still in a temper, she screamed at Ah Kong and the men to get the truck so that they could get out of here. She tried to shoo the monkeys away but they darted just a few feet forward – always out of reach – and remained where they were. They were waiting.

Without warning, while Ah Kong and the other men were getting the truck, they pounced as one on the Fat Superinendent. They were on her shoulders, on her head, little hands entangled in her hair, clinging to her arms and legs. She screamed, batting at them with her hands, kicking, trying to remove them but the monkeys clung on. One little fellow at her waist was rapidly undoing the key ring she carried. The other monkeys, keeping her fully occupied, ensured that she did not notice. Ah Kong came round one of the sheds, driving the truck straight towards her. She screamed and screamed at him.

"Stop the truck! Let me in! Kill these horrible animals. Shoot them, poison them – anything! Just get rid of them!"

The monkey at her waist had already disappeared with the keys. The others jumped off her. She clambered up into the truck as quickly as she could, shaking all over. She shrieked at Ah Kong: "Tomorrow you are to poison those pesky monkeys."

Ah Kong revved up the engine and the truck roared out of the compound. They were in such haste that they forgot to lock the gate behind them.

Once all was quiet again, several monkeys climbed up on to the perimeter fence. This was the signal for the children that all was clear. They jumped out of their hiding place and the six of them, Shirley Pooper and Bert, ran towards the compound gates.

They pushed the gates open as wide as possible and a couple of monkeys made off towards the forest. They were going to fetch the elephants and the Orang Asli.

The monkey with the keys handed them to Ibrahim. They had to act quickly. Without further ado, the children made for the first shed while Bert was already taking photographs.

Ibrahim tried several keys before he found the one that worked. Not knowing what they would find inside, they opened the door cautiously. The first thing that hit them was the awful stench. Toby and Joseph retched and Faradilla and Xin-Hui hung back. Shirley Pooper tied a handkerchief over her mouth and nose. Bert rushed in, video camera at the ready. They were shocked at what they saw: tiny cramped cages piled one on top of another, rusting, bent bars supporting the weight of bears, who were in an awful state. Bert could not see everything

until his eyes became accustomed to the dim light. Shirley had never seen or imagined anything as awful as this. She was talking rapidly into her mouthpiece.

Faradilla and Xin-Hui could not help themselves. Great tears rolled down their cheeks. Vinod wiped his eyes fiercely with his sleeve.

Ibrahim spoke to the bears, who had not seen any humans other than their torturers. The bears were frightened so Ibrahim calmed them, explaining that they were about to be rescued. He had found several smaller keys on the key ring. He guessed they were for the cages and, handing them out to Toby and Joseph, they set about trying to open the cages. Gradually, one by one, cage doors sprung open. The bears were initially too shocked to move but slowly they stirred and stuck their noses out of the prisons which had been their homes for many years. Their limbs were weak and they found movement difficult. They flexed their muscles.

Several of the bears discovered they had no muscles left. Those in the cages on top of the pile could not get down.

"Do not fret," Ibrahim told them "Help is on the way."

With their long, sensitive noses, the bears were sniffing the air. It seemed that new and unfamiliar smells assailed them from every direction. There was movement, noise, in the compound. Joseph looked out of the shed. The Orang Asli and the elephants were arriving with Hitam Malam and Hantu. The head man of the Orang Asli had not wanted Hitam Malam to come, believing he would be too distressed at what he found but Hitam Malam insisted.

Hitam Malam rushed into the shed and stopped in his tracks. He roared, a great roar of grief, and was answered by grunts and squeaks of relief from the captive bears, who, weak as they were, were delighted to see him. He padded round the shed, greeting each bear as it was released from its hellish prison.

"I am Hitam Malam, great bear of the forest. With my friends, I have come to rescue you and give you a new life. There will be no more torture, no more cruelty."

"Hail, Hitam Malam. I am Kabus Kelabu. We welcome you."

Some of the Orang Asli then came into the shed. They, too, were shocked at what they found. They helped to lift the bears from the top cages down on to the ground. Within fifteen minutes, all the bears were sitting on the ground, trying to get circulation back into their stiff and unyielding legs. Some of them, catheters trailing on the ground, managed to stagger a few steps but only a few. Several of the bears had an arm, a leg, or a paw missing. Many had broken teeth and ulcerated gums. They were thin, emaciated, and their coats grew only in patches. They all had pustulating sores on their skin where infection had set in from constant chafing against the rusty iron bars of their cages. They had been in here so long, the bears were very stinky. And they were terrified. But still, Xin-Hui and Faradilla did their best to help the bears, rubbing their legs and their backs trying to stimulate some circulation so that they could move.

The head man of the Orang Asli called Ribut into the shed. Ribut entered and lowered himself to the ground. The Orang Asli lifted the worst affected bears, two on to the stretcher Ribut was pulling and two very sick bears were carefully lifted into the panniers, which were airy and comfortable, on Ribut's back. Ribut left the shed, moving slowly and carefully. The four bears he was transporting found it impossible to believe what was happening to them. Then it was Matahari's turn and he too took on board four bears.

Like Ribut and Matahari, the other elephants lowered themselves to the ground, allowing the Orang Asli to attach stretchers and panniers to them. Even Cahaya Bulan was there, little Guruh at her side. Each elephant would be able to carry four bears through the forest. The Orang Asli carried extra stretchers on which they themselves would carry bears, four men to a stretcher. Hitam Malam insisted on pulling a stretcher behind him and so did Hantu. "These are our people, our tribe," he said. Every resource in the forest had been utilised to help the bears.

"Give us some keys, Ibrahim. We can open doors too." Xin-Hui and Faradilla held out their hands and Ibrahim gave them the keys to finish opening the cage doors in this shed. He left Toby with them while he, Joseph and Vinod went off to the second shed, followed very quickly by Shirley Pooper and Bert and, of course, Hitam Malam.

Inside the second shed, the scene was much the same as in the first. The bears were confused and bewildered. Although they hated their prison, they could not remember what was outside. Could they trust these humans? Was this a trick?

Ibrahim, Joseph and Vinod had opened all the cage doors and the Orang Asli were there, helping the bears out of their cages. The children rubbed the bears' limbs, trying to assist their circulation.

Hitam Malam padded quietly into the shed. He was weeping big wet tears as he surveyed the scene around him. He spoke to the bears:

"I am Hitam Malam, great bear of the forest."

"Hitam Malam" a bear called softly "I am Abu, once also a bear of the forest." "Abu,

Oh Abu. You will return to the forest," Hitam Malam promised.

Halilintar and Bijaksana came in and, just as Ribut and Matahari and Cahaya Bulan had done, they each carried four bears out of the shed.

Hitam Malam and Huntu bore stretchers each carrying a bear, but Hitam Malam bore a very special bear – his one-time friend, Abu.

Outside, in the compound, a few bears were finding that they were able to walk a little and the children were busily unlocking the bear cubs' cages. The cubs were in a better state than the adult bears and after a few minutes were able to scamper about.

Old Kulat was very sick. His coat was covered in fungus, ticks and mites. In many places his coat had been rubbed off by the rusty bars of his cage and he had great patches of raw, red and putrid flesh. Maggots were eating the flesh around his catheter. He had not been fed anything for the past four days since he had been put outside and was still soaked through from the rain.

Ibrahim unlocked his cage but Kulat did not move. Gently, Rambut Sutera and another of his tribe helped the old bear out and gave him water to drink. Kulat was very weak.

"I am beyond help. I cannot make the journey," he told them. "I shall die very soon. You must leave me here."

The Orang Asli dried him off, dressed his wounded, bleeding paws and gums with herbal medicines and cleaned the wound round the inserted catheter as best they could. They got rid of the maggots. They dressed the raw patches of his skin and brushed the fungus and insects out of his coat. They made a soft, dry bed for him, sheltered at the back of the compound. They left him fresh water and food including a large piece of honey comb. The honey comb was a luxury. "Take the bears. But leave me. I shall die here, but I shall now die in comfort."

Everyone took their leave of Kulat. They were sad at leaving him behind but he was right, he was too sick to move. The girls gave him a big hug, clinging to him. Even Shirley Pooper gave him a hug. The boys too gave him a hug and the Orang Asli saluted him. The elephants saluted him and Hitam Malam spent a little time with him, head nuzzling against head, allowing Kulat to lean against him and take the weight off his own feet.

Kulat could not remember ever having been as comfortable or as happy as he was now. He lay down contentedly. He was very tired.

Bert had taken a series of photographs: of Kulat in the cage, of Kulat being helped out of the cage, of Kulat having his wounds dressed by the Orang Asli and finally of Kulat lying comfortably on his soft new bed, waiting to die. He would ensure that Kulat was remembered.

The monkey troop stayed behind to keep Kulat company and to find out what the Fat Superintendent would do in the morning when she discovered the bears had all gone. They would look after Kulat to the end. They gave Hitam Malam their solemn promise.

Matahari led the way back to the forest treading carefully through the palm oil trees beside the road, followed by Cahaya Bulan and Guruh, Ribut, Halilintar and Bijaksana. Two Orang Asli walked on either side of each elephant to protect the bears on the stretchers. They were followed by Hitam Malam and Hantu, each bearing stretchers and accompanied by two Orang Asli. They moved silently through the night. Monkey scouts had been sent ahead to spot any potential danger or threat but there was none.

Eight more stretchers were borne, each carried by four Orang Asli. The cubs scampered along happily, delighted with their new found freedom. Progress through the forest would be slow. Bert ran ahead of the procession, taking photographs. The Orang Asli did not much like having their photo taken but realized it was a necessary evil. Yusof had explained to the head man that, if they got exposure, they would receive more understanding from the general public. The children and Shirley Pooper brought up the rear, frequently looking over their shoulders as they went.

Tunku and the apes were waiting anxiously, keeping a sharp lookout. Thousands of fireflies had arrived from the marshes to light the way. Joseph, Ibrahim, Toby and Vinod elected to accompany the procession through the forest. Professor Profundo, Xin-Hui and Faradilla would return to the kampong with Shirley Pooper in her car. Bert wanted to go with the procession too. He would get marvellous night shots.

Shirley and the girls got into Shirley's car. Professor Profundo came running out of the forest. He did not want to be left behind. Panting, he climbed in. Shirley drove off, heading for the kampong. They would get there before the creatures, and would wait for them.

CHAPTER 12

As soon as they arrived, without incident, at the kampong Xin-Hui and Faradilla went off in search of Yusof. They needed to tell him there would be thirty-nine adult bears and twenty cubs. Yusof scratched his head. How were they to cope with so many? All these bears would need a lot of care. He and the villagers had worked tirelessly and had made up thirty caged pens around a huge central compound which was to be exclusively for the use of the bears. The bears would be traumatised and probably too frightened to leave the security of cages for some time. Cages, after all, were all they could remember. It would take a very long time to rehabilitate them. He had put climbing frames, hollow logs and swings in the compound for the bears, so that they could play and strengthen their muscles. There were trees and shrubs, hidden dens and high platforms where the bears could rest, away from public gaze. The compound had been built right on the edge of the forest so that the wild creatures, if they wished, could come and visit the bears.

Yusof believed the bears would need simple peace and quiet as well as plenty of good food to start with. Operations, and removal of catheters and damaged gall bladders, together with repairing of fistulas could come later, once the bears were stronger. He estimated that the procession would take several hours to trek slowly through the fores, which would allow him and the villagers just enough time to build another nine or ten dens. They should be able to do it! He called a couple of villagers and they set off, prepared to work all through the night.

~

Reaching the edge of the forest without mishap, the elephants formed an orderly procession. Matahari led the way, flanked by the head man of the Orang Asli and Rambut Sutera, followed by Cahaya Bulan with Guruh trotting along beside her, then Ribut and Halilintar, followed by Hitam Malam and Hantu and the Orang Asli bearing stretchers.

Bijaksana brought up the rear. After Matahari, Bijaksana was the tallest elephant. Each stretcher was flanked by two Orang Asli, keeping an eye on the bears. Overhead in the treetops orang utan, gibbons and monkeys flew back and forth. Remarkably they were all totally silent. Fireflies danced merrily all around them lighting the way. The boys elected to march, two at the front with Matahari, and two at the back with Bijaksana.

Although the rains had stopped the forest was not yet altogether dry. The going underfoot was sometimes slippery and trees were still dripping. Every small sound was accentuated in the night. Any small jolt or bump hurt the bears who suffered in silence. They were in wonder and not quite believing what was happening to them. They scarcely moved but, noses twitching, they sniffed the air appreciatively.

Ibrahim and Joseph were fully alert, conscious of every sound and movement in the forest. The head man of the Orang Asli had told Ibrahim there was little to fear in the forest at night and no humans would venture in because of their superstitions and beliefs concerning ghosts and evil spirits but it was still pretty scary.

They journeyed quietly on, the only sounds being the creaking of rattan panniers and stretchers and heavy breathing of elephants, bears, and men exerting themselves. Shifting shadows, bats and low flying insects occasionally made Vinod jump.

"I have heard that the forest is haunted at night," he whispered to Toby. "Is is true?'

"I don't know, but it's pretty scary and spooky." Toby jumped as an owl flew past, brushing his left ear.

"Xin-Hui says there are ghosts and demons here. She says they are hungry, especially for blood."

"What does Xin-Hui know?" Toby sounded angrier than he felt. Vinod tripped. Berminyak slithered away from under his foot. "Ooh, did you see that? It was a snake."

"There's nothing there, Vinod. You're imagining it."

"I tell you, it was a snake. A huge, great, evil snake!"

Vinod moved closer to Bijaksana, walking almost under his belly. Leaves and branches brushed his face and his body as he walked, like ghostly hands caressing him. Vinod was shivering. He had no option but to keep going and he certainly was not going to say any more to Toby about his fears.

Ibrahim came to the rear of the procession.

"Vinod, Toby, we have to hide the path as we go. The Orang-Asli and the orang-utan will help us," he said. Then he started pulling branches out which were hidden in the undergrowth at the side of the path and overlaid it with these broken branches. The Orang Asli showed the boys how to brush the path clear of footprints. Tunku and Number One Son, along with their cousins, helped the boys. The hard work kept Vinod and Toby busy so that they did not have much time to think about shadows and ghosts. Looking back, Vinod thought it would be hard for anyone to follow them. He turned quickly towards the front where the fireflies danced. Behind him the forest was black as pitch.

The elephants strode slowly and purposefully on, sure-footed on the slippery ground. Occasionally a bear groaned as it was jolted. Hitam Malam and Hantu marched doggedly, determined to bear their precious charges to the kampong where they would be helped.

Suddenly the procession stopped. Matahari and the head man at the front were listening intently.

"What is it?" whispered Joseph.

Nobody answered him. They listened, straining their ears. Ibrahim crept back to the front of the procession.

"What is it?"

Joseph shrugged. Then he thought he could just make out, so faintly that he wondered if he was really hearing anything, a rumbling sound. Ibrahim heard it too. *'What is it? What can it be?'* he wondered. The sound rumbled on for about ten minutes, getting louder before it stopped. They waited in silence for another five minutes.

Finally, the head man of the Orang Asli explained

"I believe there has been a landslide up ahead. The rains have loosened rocks on the side of the hill and they have fallen down. Our path may be blocked."

Ibrahim and Joseph were dismayed. "Can we get through?" "We shall have to see."

Matahari strained at his harness and started to pull forward again, treading with caution. The others followed. Twenty minutes later they came across the landslide. At first it was difficult to see but then the fireflies flew up and hovered over it so they got a good view. The head man of the Orang Asli and Rambut

Sutera went forward and inspected the pile of rocks, stones and rubble across the path.

"We can clear a way through." called Rambut Sutera, whereupon all the Orang- Asli moved forward and with eager hands started to remove boulders and rocks. The boys joined in with gusto. And so did Tunku, Number One Son and their cousins. They unearthed a young pangolin who had a badly bruised nose and whose little foot had been crushed. They popped it into a basket to take with them to the kampong. It took a long time but finally a path had been cleared wide enough to pass through. Their relief, however, was short-lived.

"Some of the cubs are missing," Toby called. Joseph counted; there were seventeen cubs. Three were missing. *'Where can they be?'*

"They were here but must have run off when we were moving the rocks" Vinod said. "They cannot have gone far but it is so dark. It will be difficult to find them." Ibrahim was worried. The land slide had already held them up for a good hour. And now they would have to spend time searching for lost bear cubs. He looked up as Tunku approached and spoke to him. Then he smiled.

"Thank you, Tunku. That will be very helpful."

"Tunku, Number One Son and their cousins are going in search of the cubs. We are to wait here."

Tunku and Number One Son swung off into the trees, followed by their cousins. There was nothing else to be done. The boys and the Orang Asli sat down to wait. The elephants rested one leg after another, and Hitam Malam and Hantu lay down. Exhausted by the events of the night and in shock, the bile farm bears lay still on their stretchers or in their panniers. They made no attempt to move. They did not have to wait long.

Tunku came swinging back, a small squealing bear cub wrapped round his neck, followed by Number One Son with another bear cub and then a cousin with a third cub. They were all safe and sound. Bert was clicking away with his camera. He got some good shots, particularly one of Tunku swinging down through the canopy with the bear cub wrapped around his shoulders. The cubs had become disoriented in the dark and had run off in the wrong direction. The Orang Asli produced more panniers and in the interests of safety, popped every small bear cub into a pannier. Twenty more panniers to carry!

Although the bears were only half their proper weight because they were malnourished, four bears were still a lot of weight for an elephant to carry, and Hitam Malam and Hantu could carry no more. Those Orang-Asli who were not bearing stretchers took a cub each and Joseph and Ibrahim decided to share one, taking it in turns to carry it and so did Vinod and Toby. Eventually all the bear cubs had somebody to carry them.

And so the long procession marched on. *'Will we ever get to the kampong?' 'I am so tired.' 'I am so hungry.' 'How much further have we to go?'* Each boy had his own thoughts, feeling the strain of the long night. And the bear cubs seemed to be getting heavier and heavier.

Ibrahim brightened. "We are getting close to home. I recognise the surroundings. We shall soon be there."

Professor Profundo and Shirley Pooper had been waiting for them at the edge of the forest. Hearing vague sounds they crept forward, torch in hand, keeping close together. Relief and delight were written all over their faces when they spotted Matahari emerging from the darkness surrounded by tiny fireflies.

They ran forward to greet him. Then they spotted the head man of the Orang Asli, Rambut Sutera, Ibrahim and Joseph, followed by everyone else. Shirley Pooper and Professor Profundo were both weeping as they watched the bears being carried into the compound. The march had been long and it was now in the early hours of the morning.

Yusof, Aishah, the veterinary surgeons and the villagers were all there, waiting. They lined up and clapped as the dignified elephants brought in their precious loads. Many eager hands helped lift the bears gently on to the ground. Hitam Malam and Hantu came in. They too were clapped and their bears unloaded and then the Orang Asli with their stretchers came in. The bear cubs were released and ran around the compound, exploring all this new space. They quickly found Guruh, still sheltering under his mother's belly and they played together. Harnesses were removed from the elephants and from Hitam Malam and Hantu. The little pangolin was handed to one of the villagers who put aloe on his nose and found him a nice, comfortable den in which to spend the rest of the night. Yusof would look at his crushed foot later in the morning, when it would be light.

The elephants and the Orang-Asli departed, leaving the compound full of sick and bewildered bears. Tunku, Number One Son and their tribe departed. Hitam Malam and Hantu stayed. They went from bear to bear, reassuring them and explaining that they were now free.

Those bears who could not walk were carried carefully to cages packed with straw where food and water were waiting for them. Those who could walk were led slowly to their cages. They staggered, they wobbled but they made it. The cubs shared two dens between them and snuggled gratefully up to each other. The bears would be left to sleep for the rest of the night. Hitam Malam and Hantu did not leave the compound. They elected to stay overnight in case the rescued bears needed further reassurance. For tonight, no more could be done.

The villagers went home. Shirley Pooper and Bert rattled off in Shirley's old jalopy, while Yusof, Aishah, Professor Profundo and the children headed for Yusof's house where, within minutes, they were all fast asleep. The baby monkey curled up on Faradilla's pillow and Katak lay at her feet.

CHAPTER 13

As dawn crept in there was neither sound nor movement in the bear compound at the Forest Sanctuary. All was still. Yusof, concerned for his new charges, was making an early morning check. He could hear the sound of snoring from a few of the cages. He smiled wryly to himself. *'This was probably the first proper night's sleep they have had in years.'* Hitam Malam and Hantu, exhausted after the night's hard work, were fast asleep, curled up together, guarding the sick bears.

Yusof, content, returned to the house for breakfast. The day ahead was to be another day of hard work. He and Aishah shared breakfast, a rare luxury to be alone together before Professor Profundo and the children awoke. Yusof then headed off for the bear compound. There was a lot to do.

When Professor Profundo and the children emerged later, bleary-eyed and sleepy, Aishah told them that Yusof had already gone to the compound where work with the bears was to start immediately. She told them that the bears would still be terrified. After all, they had known nothing but fear and pain for years. And humans were the perpetrators of their pain and suffering. She also explained gently that some of the bears might have to be put down if their suffering was found to be too great to be relieved. The bears would take time to adjust.

They would have to learn new behaviour patterns. In other words, they would have to learn to be bears, rather than objects in cages. It would be a long, slow process. But the children were not disheartened. They gobbled up their breakfast and rushed down to the compound to help.

The two veterinary surgeons had arrived and they and Yusof were preparing an operating theatre, disinfecting and sterilising it. But before any of the bears could be operated on, Yusof explained, they would have to be washed very gently and thoroughly, dried off with towels and then left to dry out thoroughly in the sun. Then their wounds and sores would have to be dressed. Perhaps the children might like to help with washing the bears, he suggested. They agreed enthusiastically. They hoped to operate on all the bears within the next forty-eight hours.

"But just now they have to be fed. The food is prepared and ready. Can you go and take it to the bears?" Yusof asked them. The children rushed off to do his bidding.

Hitam Malam and Hantu were awake. Ibrahim gave them their breakfast first. They ate ravenously and gratefully. Hitam Malam explained to Ibrahim that soon he and Hantu would be going off into the forest to find the mothers of the bear cubs and bring them here to be reunited with their babies. But first he and Hantu would help Ibrahim encourage the bears to come out of their dens into the sunshine and be washed.

Slowly, one by one, the children, Hitam Malam and Hantu coaxed the sick bears out of their dens. They placed food for them a little way outside each den, encouraging the bears to come out and eat.

The first bear to venture out into the sunlight was Abu, who had known Hitam Malam of old and who now placing his trust in

Hitam Malam, overcame his fear. He dragged himself forward slowly, painfully, limping on three legs. The fourth appeared useless. He just dragged it along. His paws, raw flesh, were sore and bleeding where, in the intense pain of being milked for bile, he had chewed them until they bled. A catheter trailed on the ground beneath him. In the sunlight Hitam Malam and Ibrahim could see how dirty, dusty, emaciated and scabby Abu was. In contrast, Hitam Malam was fat, sleek, and glossy. Ibrahim turned away quickly, tears stinging his eyes.

Joseph and Toby approached slowly, carrying buckets of warm, soapy water and great big sponges. They did not want to frighten Abu any further. Vinod, Xin-Hui and Faradilla carried towels, brushes, combs, and salves for his sores. Exhausted, Abu lay down in the sunlight and allowed the boys to sponge him down with the warm, soapy water. Xin-Hui and Faradilla gently teased the knots and dead insects out of his coat before applying soothing salve to his sores, then they left him to sleep for a while in the sun and moved on to the next brave bear to emerge. Every time one of the children moved, the poor bear winced, as if she was expecting them to hit her or hurt her. It was Chio-Bu. As she slumped to the ground, Faradilla sat at her head and stroked her and after the boys had washed her thoroughly, Xin-Hui combed and brushed her coat.

Other bears were emerging from their cages, emboldened by the sight of Abu and Chio Bu being cleaned and comforted. And in turn they too were bathed and groomed. They were all in a sorry state but already felt more comfortable once they had been cleaned and brushed.

Yusof and the two veterinary surgeons came to see them. He explained to Ibrahim that today they would only remove the catheters, and possibly gall bladders too, from those bears who were strongest and that they would be given a light tranquilising anaesthetic before they were carried to the operating room. Hitam Malam joined Ibrahim and said that he would tell the bears what was about to happen. The bears were incredulous. Their catheters, the source of so much agony, were about to be removed? They took Abu first. He was placed carefully on a stretcher and carried off.

Yusof, the veterinary surgeons, village helpers and the children worked hard all day long cleaning up the bears, trying to give them comfort. Yusof and the surgeons operated that day on Abu, Chio Bu, and three other bears. Two of the bears had cancers which were too far advanced and they were in such tremendous pain that Yusof could do nothing to relieve them. So instead, he sent them to their heavenly lairs where they would be at rest and at peace for ever. Abu, Chio Bu and the other bear were returned to their cages where Hitam Malam and Hantu watched over them.

The following day was much the same as the last day, the children were so busy they did not notice time passing. The parents arrived to help. Each set of parents was assigned a bear of their own to wash and clean.

Thy children believed Shirley Pooper had gone back to the offices of The South East Asia Gazette, where she was going to write up her article. Bert had gone with her. He had lots of photographs he wanted to develop. But they both said they would be back.

Xin-Hui and Faradilla giggled when they thought of Shirley Pooper. They remembered her as she had been when they first met her – long, red fingernails, bright red lipstick, frizzy hair like a scarecrow, tight skirt and very high heels. But now when she was with the children, she dressed sensibly for the occasion. She wore khaki slacks, a long-sleeved shirt, and walking boots. She tied her hair back, cut her nails shorter and wore no make-up at all.

"She looks a lot better, lah!" Xin-Hui laughed.

There was a commotion on the edge of the forest. Hitam Malam and Hantu were there, agitated. Tunku had arrived and with him was the leader of the macaque troop. Ibrahim went to see what was happening. The little monkey was chattering animatedly, jumping up and down, waving its arms in the air. Tunku sat on the ground, one long arm wrapped around his head, as if he could scarcely bear to hear what the monkey was telling him. Hitam Malam, very distressed, was weaving his head from side to side and Hantu just stood with his head hanging down, a picture of total dejection as Joseph approached them.

"What's going on, Ibrahim?"

"Sshh! The monkey's talking. I shall tell you in a minute."

Finally the monkey stopped his chattering and sat, still and quiet, beside Tunku. Tunku did not stir. Hitam Malam and Hantu sat down. They were crying and so was Ibrahim.

"What's up? What's the matter?" Joseph pulled at his sleeve.

"It is Kulat. He is dead." Ibrahim answered simply. "Shirley Pooper and Bert were there, hiding. They saw everything."

"What do you mean, they were there? They went home."

"No. They did not. They went back to the bile farm compound to see what would happen the morning after we rescued the bears."

In the offices of The South East Asia Gazette, Sam was exultant. Shirley Pooper and Bert had done it again. They had another scoop.

Shirley was typing up her notes.

"But I am not going to let this go to print yet," she told Sam. "I need to tell the children first what has happened to old Kulat."

"Old who?"

"Oh, never mind, Sam. You'll just have to trust me for another day. And then, I promise you, you'll have your scoop."

Sam knew Shirley was stubborn, but she was also infuriating – only half stories, half truths, until she was ready. But he could not afford to upset her; she was too valuable. She had promised him a six-page insert for the Sunday paper.

"O.K. Shirley, in your own time!"

"Have you got those photos ready, Bert?" Shirley called.

"Give me five minutes."

"I want to get across to the kampong and tell the children about Kulat. If you can bring the photos, that would be good."

"Five minutes, as I said." "Good!"

Shirley began gathering up her papers. Sam still had no idea what her 'scoop' was about. That was Shirley's way. She never told him anything until it was all ready for print. She was such a frustrating woman!

CHAPTER 14

Shirley Pooper and Bert rattled and bumped their way down the road into the kampong where they parked the car and then made their way towards the Sanctuary.

"Listen up, children," she called. "We have some news for you."

The children stopped what they were doing and came over to Shirley and Bert.

"Sit down" she said. "You are not going to like this but you need to know before it goes into the papers tomorrow."

"When we left you the other night, Bert and I got a couple of hours' sleep, and then we went back to the bear bile farm. We wanted to see what would happen when the Fat Superintendent and her men returned. I'll tell you everything exactly as it happened. Bert will put me right if I get anything wrong.

We went back and we hid in one of the outbuildings. We had a good view of the whole compound from there. But first we shut the barn doors and replaced the padlocks, so that it would not be immediately obvious the bears had been released. Then we threw the keys away as far as we could into the palm oil plantation.

Old Kulat was lying in his nest, happy as it was possible for him to be. I gave him a cuddle and he seemed to appreciate it. He had some carrots and bananas and honey for breakfast. The macaques were everywhere, keeping an eye on things. One of them, sitting on the fence, gave us a warning that a lorry was approaching with the Fat Superintendent and her henchmen.

The lorry rolled into the compound (remember that they had left the gates ajar the previous evening). At first, they did not notice anything was different. The Fat Superintendent was too engrossed in trying to find her lost keys. She shouted at Ah Kong as if it was his fault that she had lost them and at the other men. It was a good ten minutes before Ah Kong noticed that the bear cubs were missing. He shouted and the Fat Superintendent came running. Then they noticed that Kulat's cage was empty. They were calling out and running around like headless chickens but still they could not find the missing keys. And they did not see Kulat in the shadows. Kulat just stayed very still but he was watching everything.

I think the Fat Superintendent then noticed how quiet the compound was. She shouted at Ah Kong to break the padlocks on the barn doors with his axe. He and the other two men started hammering and banging at the padlocks until the barn doors flew open. It took them quite a while. They went inside and then we heard a great wailing noise. The Fat Superintendent was wailing and screeching. She rushed out of the first barn and into the second, then she came out of that one, yelling, beating her chest, pulling at her hair. Ah Kong and the other three men were running around looking for the bears. It was total chaos."

Shirley giggled. She could not help herself.

"Then the Fat Superintendent spotted some of the Macaques. Actually, I was afraid she might find us but she didn't. 'It's all their fault, those devils,' she screamed. 'Kill them. Shoot them'. We were concerned for the monkeys but we need not have worried. They were far too fast for Ah Kong and his guys.

They were blundering about not knowing which way to turn, what to do, when the Fat Superintendent went to her office. Her ledger was missing too. The monkeys had taken it. She screamed so much, I think she fainted."

Shirley and Bert were both giggling now.

"Bert got some beautiful shots. Ah Kong and his men carried her out into the middle of the compound where they lay her down on her back. Her big belly stuck up in the air like a tank turret. Ah Kong tried to fan her with an old newspaper but it didn't work so they poured a bucket of water over her. You should have heard the screams and seen her scramble to sit up!"

Shirley and Bert were laughing so much, they doubled up. Their laughter was infectious. The children could not help joining in. The picture Shirley painted of the Fat Superintendent was just too much.

"Anyway, when she eventually got to her feet - and it was quite a struggle - she was a bit quieter. I think the cold water gave her a bit of a shock. Unfortunately, she then noticed old Kulat's cage was mssing from the middle of the compound. 'Where is Kulat?' she asked 'He cannot have gone far. Find Kulat. I want him alive.' So they spread out, looking in a more organised manner this time." Shirley was grave now as she spoke. "Kulat did not wait for them to find him. He came to them. I don't know how he did it, where he found the strength, but that wonderful old bear dragged himself out of the shadows. I thought he couldn't walk but he was walking on all fours, heading straight for them, growling, showing his teeth.

The macaques were magnificent. They were everywhere, getting in the way, tripping the men up, being as much of a nuisance as they could.

'Cut off his paws. Get the axe.' the Fat Superintendent was screaming at Ah Kong. They were all running towards him. Kulat raised himself up on to his hind legs. He must have stood over six feet tall. Reaching down, with seemingly no effort, he pulled the catheter out of his own body. It must have really hurt but he was impervious to the pain. The catheter stuck to his flesh and in pulling it out he tore a great hole in his belly. Blood and guts poured out. Blood was spurting everywhere - the wound was so big that even his entrails fell out.

Raising his front paws, claws extended, beyond pain, he rushed at the Fat

Superintendent and the others. He was roaring and growling, pulling his lips back to reveal his teeth. He moved so fast! Tall and strong, he charged them. Ah Kong raised his rifle and shot him. Still Kulat pressed on roaring defiantly. Ah Kong shot him again and Kulat kept going. Ah Kong shot him again, and again. The Fat Superintendent was screaming to hack off his paws with the axe. One of the other men tried to approach Kulat but he swept him away, gashing the man's side with his claws. He picked one man up and threw him through the air. He was almost on top of the Fat Superintendent. I think he would have killed her. But Ah Kong fired one more shot, and Kulat fell. He fell right on top of the Fat Superintendent. She was smothered in guts and gore. The monkeys had all stopped rushing about. Bert and I could not move, we were so shocked by what we had seen. But Bert had taken lots of photos. We have all the evidence. Kulat is safe now in his bear heaven and they did not get his paws."

Shirley, Bert and the children were all silent. They had not noticed Yusof approach. He was silent too.

"Brave Kulat! I wish I had given him a bigger cuddle," Faradilla eventually managed to say through choking sobs.

Shirley went on. "Ah Kong was shocked, I think, and the Fat Superintendent was struggling underneath Kulat to get out. Finally she emerged red-faced, covered with blood and gore and weeping uncontrollably. She was absolutely hysterical. Ah Kong bundled her and the other two wounded men - I think one has a broken back - on to the lorry, and they went off."

"I do not think, Shirley, that you should print this story until after the bears we have rescued have been operated on, and are safe."

"But Yusof..."

"I mean it, Shirley. Our first concern has to be for the safely of the remaining bears and I do believe that the Fat Superintendent and Ah Kong will not give up easily."

"Well, if you say so. But I MUST be allowed to go to print within the next few days." "I give you my solemn promise, Shirley. You will be able to."

Bert sniffed hard. "I want to give that bear a decent burial. I have never seen such bravery. There he was, a poor, sick bear, too

sick to live and he went out blazing in glory."
"I shall never forget that bear."

"I think we should name the bear enclosure
"The Kulat Enclosure" intervened Yusof. "If
you have good enough photos, Bert, I know
a man, a real craftsman who lives in the
kampong.

He makes exquisite wooden sculptures and
I know he will make a sculpture of Kulat for
us so that he will always be remembered. We
can place the sculpture in the middle of the
compound. That would be a fitting memorial."

The boys, Xin-Hui and Faradilla could not
speak. The girls had tears rolling down their
cheeks and Vinod kept brushing his face with
his hand. They all had big lumps in their
throats but they thought Yusof's idea was a
great idea. Ibrahim knew what had happened
of course. The monkey had told him although
not so graphically. He looked across at the
bear enclosure but Hitam Malam and Hantu
had gone, together with Tunku and the little
macaque. He wondered vaguely where they
were.

CHAPTER 15

Shirley Pooper and Bert stayed on at the the Forest Sanctuary. Shirley wanted more material for her story as she wanted to finish it. She envisaged a weekly serial, perhaps. *'Sam will like that'* she thought. *'People will want to buy the newspaper for each instalment.'* Bert, as ever, wandered about taking photographs and Shirley was talking into her little microphone. Shirley interviewed Yusof, who showed her the extent of the bear's wounds and infections. He told her that he felt some of the bears' infections were too far advanced and he had already put two to sleep.

Then Shirley Pooper and Bert left. They went off in the old car, bumping along merrily. But they did not go to the offices of the South East Asia Gazette. They took a left turn in the road and headed off for the bile farm compound. Bert felt he had one more task to do. In the back of the car he had a couple of large spades and shovels and some nice clean linen. He was going to take that bear into the forest and give it a decent burial, if it was the last thing he did.

The compound was empty when they arrived. Not a soul about! A small macaque greeted them. He had remained to keep watch. But Kulat's body was not there either. They searched and searched but could not find it. Bert picked up an old file which he thought might reveal something interesting or useful.

"You know, Bert" Shirley said "I think there's something fishy here. That Ah Kong's a nasty piece of work, and I don't believe he'd leave the evil palm oil baron's employment. He was too deeply in his pocket."

"Uuhmm!" Bert answered. He was still looking for Kulat's body or some sign of where it might be. There was no freshly dug earth in the compound - nothing.

"Perhaps they have taken his body away on the lorry."

"No. I don't think so. Why should they? They couldn't use it, even for meat. He was too diseased. And they don't strike me as compassionate people. Perhaps we'd better leave. I don't like it here. It's an evil place, a sad place."

"Yeah! Let's get out of here."

So climbing back into Shirley's little car, they left.

That night Matahari, Ribut, Halilintar and Bijaksana gathered at the edge of the forest. They were nervous yet determined. They did not like to leave the safety of the forest. There was a full moon and the skies were bright multitudes of twinkling stars. They waited until they were sure the coast was clear. Then, lolloping along at a good pace, ears flapping, tails held high, they made for the bile farm compound, that terrible place of hell. It was deserted under the starry sky.

Working as a team, the elephants bulldozed down the fences, they bulldozed down the outbuildings and then they tackled the big barns. Heaving and straining, they flattened them. They tossed the rusting old cages about, gored them with their gleaming white tusks and trampled them.

For a further couple of hours they trampled everything in sight - flattening, destroying. When they turned, as one, and left there was nothing there. They padded quietly back into the forest. Only the little guardian macaque and the stars had witnessed their destruction. The little guardian macaque could now go home.

The elephants were only just in time. The next morning the Fat Superintendent, Ah Kong and two of his henchmen (the third was in hospital with a broken back) arrived in the old truck closely followed by the Baron in his smart new car. They were dumbfounded. What had happened to the bile farm? Everything had gone. All that was left was flattened earth. The Fat Superintendent and Ah Kong were in a state of shock. The Baron lost his temper completely.

"What have you done?" he screamed at the Fat Superintndent. "I had a lot of money vested in this bile farm. Where are the bears? Where are the buildings? Where are the ledgers?" The Fat Superintendent had nothing to say. She cringed. What could she say? She had no idea what had happened.

The Baron turned to Ah Kong. "Ah Kong, what have you got to say for yourself?" Ah Kong could not answer. He, the Fat Superintendent and the two henchmen stood there, heads hanging down, crestfallen. *'What has happened? It is a mystery.'* It was a mystery to all of them.

"You are fired!" screamed the Baron. "All of you. And do not expect to get any wages. You will not."

And with that, he flounced into his car and, revving the engine, tore out of the compound or rather, out of the space which had once been a compound. He was in a rage. *'This is not the end. I shall get to the bottom of this.'* he muttered to himself as he wrestled with the steering wheel.

It took five long days to clean up, soothe and operate on all the adult bears. Two more had terribly advanced cancer and Yusof put them to sleep – sending them to their own special heavenly lair where they would be at peace for ever. Many had their gall bladders removed altogether, they were so infected. Several had rotting limbs amputated and rotting teeth and claws removed. Many had their catheters removed. Others had to be cleaned and stitched. After the operations, they were placed in big, comfortable cages in a light and airy place. The cage floors were solid and covered with great mounds of comfortable clean straw. They had room in their cages to move and to walk around if they wanted to. The children tended the bears daily, feeding them, grooming them, dressing their wounds. Slowly, very slowly, the bears gained confidence. But it was hard for them to overcome their fear. That would take a very, very long time. Yusof said that above all else, the bears needed to rest.

Hitam Malam and Hantu had been gone for several days. One morning, early, there they were on the edge of the compound with six strange bears. It was quite a shock for Joseph to see them there. Joseph had been busy gathering fresh vegetables for the sick bears but he rushed off to fetch Ibrahim. When Ibrahim arrived Hitam Malam told him that two of these bears were the mothers of some of the cubs and the other four bears were willing to adopt the remaining cubs. Ibrahim opened the gate to the compound where the bear cubs were still living. Yusof had checked every one of them and apart from being too thin and scraggy, they were fit. The cubs were all asleep, snuggled up in their dens.

Ibrahim led Orkid and Hadiah, the two surviving mothers, to the dens. Beside themselves with anxiety, they pushed their long snouts into the dens, grunting loudly, pawing the ground, feverishly trying to get at the cubs. The sleepy cubs awoke and tumbled out of the dens.

Joseph, Toby, Vinod and the girls had arrived. They stood around the edge of the compound and watched. The girls were a little in awe of all these big wild bears. They were very black and sleek, and had beautiful yellow moon crescents emblazoned on their chests.

Some of the cubs started squealing wildly, running from bear to bear. Overcome with excitement, they were recognising their mothers. Within only a few minutes, Orkid and Hadiah were surrounded by their own little families. Hitam Malam was crying big tears of joy, the little cubs were squealing, Orkid and Hadiah were crying big tears of gratitude, and the children were certainly all crying big tears. It was a very soggy occasion.

"But, look," cried Faradilla, pointing, "the other cubs are still left." Huddled together at the edge of a den were fifteen forlorn little bear cubs. "They look so sad. Where are their Mummies?"

The children looked around. None of these females seemed to know the cubs. Ibrahim spoke to Hitam Malam.

"Hitam Malam believes they may be the cubs of those bears who were killed." he said.

"Poor little cubs, without any Mummies." Xin-Hui rushed up to them, scooping one up in her arms to give it a cuddle. Faradilla was close on her heels and Vinod also scooped up a cub and gave it a cuddle. They did not notice Hitam Malam moving from one deliriously happy bear family to another, to the other bears and then across to Ibrahim.

"Hitam Malam says these other four bears will happily adopt the cubs and bring them up as their own. That is what they came here for."

"Oh, can we not keep them, lah?"

"No, Xin-Hui, you know what Bapa says. We can only keep those creatures who are no longer able to fend for themselves."

"But the bear cubs cannot help themselves."

"These Mummies are willing to adopt them. That is the best thing," Ibrahim said firmly.

One of the females, as if to reinforce what Ibrahim had said, moved across to one of the forlorn cubs, nuzzled it and then, picking it up gently in her mouth, she carried it back to where she had been standing on the edge of the forest and deposited it. She returned to fetch another cub, and another. The other three remaining females followed suit.

"There!" Ibrahim was triumphant. "Every one of the cubs has a Mummy."

"It's for the best, Xin-Hui. Look how happy they are." Joseph and Toby were watching the cubs gambolling happily around the adult bears and the mothers were playing - really playing

- with the cubs.

Hitam Malam conferred with Ibrahim. He told him that he, Hitam Malam and Hantu had returned to the bile farm in the dead of night and with Matahari's help they had removed old Kulat's body. They had taken it back to the forest where he always belonged. He then turned and led the way out of the compound, followed by the six bears and their cubs. Hantu brought up the rear. They made their way into the forest but just before they disappeared out of sight, the bears turned as one and looked at the children. In their own inimitable way they were saying "good-bye" and "thank-you."

"It is very lonely here without the cubs" Vinod felt desolate.

"Yes, it is," said Ibrahim. "But it is for the best. They will grow into fine bears and have cubs of their own." Ibrahim was being particularly firm to hide his own disappointment that they had gone. Over the past few days the cubs had been an endless source of fun and pleasure to the children.

"Come on . We still have work to do." Joseph said, making his way back to the vegetable patch. Vinod and Toby had been in the middle of changing bears' bedding and Ibrahim had been helping his father measure out the medicines, while the girls had been cleaning out water bowls and giving the bears clean water to drink. Life at the Forest Sanctuary had become routine after their adventure.

Yusof said the caged bears would be released into the compound as soon as their wounds had completely healed. Some would take longer to heal than others but he anticipated that he could start releasing some of the bears within the next couple of days. They were recovering from their operations very quickly, and had even started to put on weight. Adjusting would be a problem for many of them 'though, particularly those whose limbs had been amputated.

Abu fell into this category. Yusof had no option but to amputate the dead leg he had been dragging along.

"Why was his leg like that?" Ibrahim had asked.

"It probably goes back to when he was caught in a trap. The trap has big steel teeth which would cut right into a small bear's leg, often shattering the bone as well. He must have been in great pain. Once the blood circulation stops, the leg dies."

"How will he manage without a leg?"

"I have an idea." Yusof had said. He had amputated legs from fifteen bears. "But, in the meantime, there is a lot of work to be done. We have our Grand Opening Ceremony the day after tomorrow. And we have to make sure everything is ready for that."

CHAPTER 16

Ibrahim was having a few minutes rest. Lying on his back in the shade he was overtly watching the bears in the cages. They did not move about much, but kept themselves snuggled up tight in one place, usually a corner. They slept a lot. He spent every spare minute he had watching the bears.

"They DO have different personalities," he had told his father. "You just have to watch them carefully to find out."

Sadly Yusof had warned Ibrahim that probably some of the bears would never recover mentally. Their behaviour patterns would be strange and they would always need help.

"That does not matter, Bapa, now that we have the Sanctuary up and running."

"But we still have to raise money on a regular basis. If we cannot, The Sanctuary will not survive."

Ibrahim was thinking about that conversation with his father. He must speak to Joseph and the others.

Shirley Pooper and Bert were back in the offices of the South East Asia Gazette. Shirley was typing away frantically. She had a lot to tell. Bert was preparing photographs. He wanted to use only the most graphic photos, the most disturbing ones. Sadly he had many of them. Shirley had shut the door very firmly on Sam, the editor. He was hopping about outside her office, itching to discover what she was writing about.

"To the Rescue Again. The Doughty Warriors Save the Bears!" was the headline. It took Shirley a few hours but finally she was satisfied with her article. She emerged from her office, clutching sheaves of type-written pages.

"There, Sam. What do you think?"

Sam read in silence for several minutes. Then he went back over the article again. "Shirley. It's a good story, a very good story. But we can't go to print with this. Those children stole the bears. That's what this story is telling me. They will be prosecuted for theft."

"But Sam, the bears were stolen from the forest in the first place. They were there - in that horrible place - illegally."

"Can you prove it, Shirley? Can you provide the evidence?" Shirley was devastated. Sam was right.

"Bert, Bert!" she called. "We can't go to print. The children will be prosecuted for theft, Sam says. We need to provide evidence that the bears were stolen from the forest. How can we do that?"

"Shirley, I'm sure there's a way. Don't worry! If we can't go to print today it doesn't matter. We've got the opening of the Forest Sanctuary in a couple of days. That will give you more to write about and it will give me some more photos and we can think about it in the meantime."

"But we've only got the word of the children. Ibrahim says the animals talk to him and I believe it, but that won't be accepted in a court of law."

"Shirley, we'll think of something." Bert was very positive. "After all, you've never let anything get the better of you yet, Shirley Pooper." He gave her a big hug.

'Good old Bert. What would I do without him?' she thought. "You're right, Bert." Shirley sighed. There was no more she could do for the time being.

Faradilla was playing with her new playmate, the baby monkey.

"You must find his Mummee, lah! You cannot keep him. That would not be fair." Xin-Hui knew how attached Faradilla became to her little rescued friends.

"I know. I shall really try after the big Opening of the Sanctuary. But I shall miss him when he goes." Faradilla sighed.

CHAPTER 17

"We have only twenty-four hours left and so much to do!" "Will a lot of people be coming?"

"Bapa hopes so. The more popular the Sanctuary becomes, the more money he can raise to help the creatures. Bapa says that Shirley Pooper's boss, Sam, has put a big advertisement in the paper for us."

"Do you know who is coming?"

"Not really. But that nice Prime Minister is coming. You know, the one who invited us to dinner after the great fight; the one who has the lovely washroom for ladies."

"What will you wear?"

"Oh, that pink sarong and matching kebayah which Mama embroidered. It is my favourite. Ow!" The little monkey on Faradilla's shoulder was pulling her hair.

"I got a lovely new blue dress for the Chinese New Year; it's peacock blue. I shall wear that." Xin-Hui said decisively. "What are you going to do with him?" she pointed at the baby monkey clinging now to Faradilla's back. "Are you going to try and find his Mummee?"

Faradilla looked crestfallen. "I suppose I have to."

"Well, you have not done much about it yet. You ought to. Your Bapa will tell you that the longer you leave it, the harder it gets." Xin-Hui was being very stern.

Faradilla sighed. "You are right, Xin-Hui. Come on. Let's go and help put the bunting up." The girls ran off to join the boys. The little monkey still clung, limpet-like, to Faradilla's back.

The whole kampong was a hive of activity. After all, everyone who lived here would be involved in this Sanctuary for sick and injured creatures. Most families would have at least one member working at the Sanctuary, and Yusof had deliberately kept them all involved at every stage of its development. He desperately needed their support.

A huge marquee had been put up and inside it rows of little gilt chairs with red cushions had been placed below a great big dais from which Yusof and the Prime Minister would make speeches. The ladies of the village were decorating the dais with wreaths of flowers and vines, and tables had been placed all round the marquee. They were decorated with flowers and little tea lights. All the food would be served from these tables.

Outside the carpenters were putting the finishing touches to the wooden classroom and science room they had built. Ladies in the Information Centre were putting out leaflets and samples of vegetation and foliage. And the ladies manning the tea room were busy cooking and baking. Aishah was tending the beehives, ensuring they were at their very best for this big day.

Men from the village were putting up the bunting. Standing at the top of long ladders, they still had to stretch as high as they could. They told the children they could not help here. They were not tall enough. Yusof sent them off to clean out the bear compound and make sure it was absolutely ready for the bears. Not that many bears would be in it for the Grand Opening! He thought that one or two might just be able to go out for an hour or so but it would be a big ordeal for them. They still preferred the safety of their cages.

The bears' cages were spotless - the bears themselves were beginning to put on weight already and their coats were improving but many of them still had bandages on. Some even had drips attached to them, they were so weak. Yusof had insisted that the bear cages were not to be open to the public. The experience of being peered at would be too traumatic for the sick bears. The compound was green and fresh with a big pond in the middle; climbing frames, logs and platforms were in place and lots of dens and shady places had been provided. The far side of the compound was right on the edge of the forest so that forest creatures could come and visit the bears in the compound without humans being aware of their presence.

The monitor lizard and several other lizards, the pangolins, monkeys and gibbons, the civet cats, the flying squirrel, bats and birds, snakes, slow loris, insects, and many others now had their own brand new enclosures, which were spotless and could be easily viewed without disturbing the creatures. There were information panels on every enclosure, telling the public all about the creatures.

Aishah's gardens were beautifully tended, with not a weed in sight. They too would be open to the public. Each different species of plant had a little stake by it with a notice telling people all about the plant and its properties. Professor Profundo was looking after this aspect of the Sanctuary for Aishah. He was having a lovely time writing out the information on the stakes. Lovingly, he watered the plants for her. She was raising some very rare species here and they needed tender loving care. He looked after them like babies.

Ibrahim, on the far side of the bears' compound, was bending down pulling up weeds when he became aware of a presence. He stood up. There was Number One Son, watching him from high up in the branches of a tree.

"Number One Son" he called. "How are you? When are you to have your Naming Day? We are to have the Grand Opening of the Sanctuary tomorrow, which is why we are all so busy. Come down and talk to me."

Number One Son swung down from the tree. He gave Ibrahim a big hug, which was reciprocated.

"That is what I came to tell you." he said. "My Naming Day is to be in three days' time. I would like you to be there."

"I would not miss it for anything. And the others will come too, I promise. Will you be coming to our Opening Ceremony?"

"A number of us will be watching but you humans may not see us."

"Oh, that is alright. It will just be good to know that you are there. How are Tunku and Puteri and Number Two Son?"

"They are fine, preparing for the Naming Day. You will see them then."

Ibrahim laughed. "All this preparing! There is so much of it. But I am sure it is worth it in the end."

The following day dawned fair and fine. Joseph, Vinod and Xin-Hui were delivered bright and early to the kampong by their parents. They went straight down to the Sanctuary. All the creatures had to be fed and watered and made absolutely spick and span for this great day. By

10.30 a.m., chores finished, the children rushed back to Yusof's house where Aishah had prepared a hasty breakfast of roti prata, after which they showered and cleaned up before donning their best clothes. Aishah helped Faradilla and Xin-Hui, brushing their hair until it gleamed and lacing fresh flowers into it. Both the girls looked adorable, Faradilla in pink sarong and kabaya, and Xin-Hui in a peacock blue cheong-sam. Ibrahim wore a traditional beja melayu, shirt and trousers, with a short sarong over. He looked very smart. Joseph and Toby, being European, wore smart trousers and white shirts. Professor Profundo chose a scarlet shirt and white trousers. He looked very colourful. Yusof and Aishah also wore traditional dress for this special day.

"They are so beautiful. I wish I could wear Malagian costume." sighed Xin-Hui.

Early in the morning Ibrahim and Joseph had let Abu, Chio Bu, and Kabus Kelabu out into the bear compound. They were the only bears who were up to it. They were nervous, but excited too. It was a long time since any of them had walked on grass, had smelled clean air or felt the warmth of the sun on their backs. They lay down in the middle of the compound, close to the pond, and revelled in the warm sun.

In the marquee, the ladies of the kampong, all in sarongs and kebaya and with flowers in their shiny black hair, were busily putting up last-minute decorations of flowers and greenery. The men also wore traditional dress. Everything and everyone looked splendid.

At 11.30 a.m. precisely, when the gate was opened, people were already queuing, eager to get in. A steady stream of people poured through the gate from then on. The parents arrived.

They had been allocated special seats on the dais alongside Professor Profundo, Aishah and the children. They too were wearing their best clothes. Mrs Singh looked particularly resplendent in a new emerald green and gold sari. Shirley Pooper and Bert arrived, with all Bert's photographic paraphernalia, which he immediately set about erecting. Yusof waited patiently. There was a commotion at the gate. The Prime Minister had arrived. Professor Profundo rose with alacrity and made his way to the gate.

"My Dear Teo! How lovely to see you again. And under such auspicious circumstances." he cried, shaking the Prime Minister warmly by the hand.

Teo, equally pleased to see his dear friend, the Professor, shook his hand heartily. "Professor Profundo, my dear Professor! We have some catching up to do. But what a fine day it is today and what a fine thing Yusof is doing." He beamed at the Professor. Bert was snapping away with his camera. The Prime Minister was genuinely very fond of his friend, Professor Profundo. He was also aware of the good publicity this Sanctuary opening would bring him. Professor Profundo led the Prime Minister to the dais where Yusof was waiting. The marquee was filling up rapidly.

"So many people, lah!" exclaimed Xin-Hui, looking around her. Then she gasped "I think Ah Kong is here!"

"What! Where!" Hearts racing, pounding against their rib cages, Joseph, Vinod and Ibrahim were scanning the crowds.

"At the back, over there, with that ugly fat woman and the fat man with a shiny face."

"Ah, that is the Fat Superintendent I saw at the bile farm," Vinod breathed softly. He was the only one of them who had actually seen the Fat Superintendent – apart from Shirley Pooper and Bert.

"Where is Shirley Pooper? We need to find her. She has seen both the Fat Superintendent and the Evil Palm Oil Baron." Joseph did not know why he mentioned the Evil Palm Oil Baron; perhaps it was just instinct. But the hackles were standing up on the back of his neck and that was always a bad sign.

Shirley Pooper was approaching the dais. She wanted to get close so she could record Yusof's speech. She was looking very smart today. The usually untidy and unkempt Shirley Pooper was wearing shiny high heels, a straight skirt and a crisp blouse and her hair was tied back in a neat roll. She was wearing make-up too and her nails were painted, but not the horrible vermilion she had used when the children first met her. She was determined not to say anything to the children about Sam's belief that they had stolen the bears. She would keep that to herself. She had made Bert promise to say nothing either.

"Shirley! Shirley!" Toby, who was nearest to the edge of the dais, whispered. "Joseph wants you."

She looked up. "What is it, Joseph?"

"Is that the Fat Superintendent and the Evil Palm Oil Baron at the back with Ah Kong?" "Where?" Shirley was craning her neck to see. Then she spotted them. She stared for a moment, then exclaimed, "Yes, that's them! What are they doing here? They can't be up to any good." Her suspicions had been right. The Fat Superintendent and Ah Kong were working for the Evil Palm Oil Baron. Shirley was worried. What if they were going to accuse the children of having stolen their bears? What if they were to make a public announcement?

"I knew the Evil Palm Oil Baron was behind Ah Kong and that Fat Superintendent. I just knew it!" Joseph was breathing hard.

"I thought he was in prison."

"He got out early for good behaviour. Bert and I suspected he might be involved but we couldn't prove it." Shirley said.

Ah Kong, the Fat Superintendent and the Evil Palm Oil Baron were shuffling their feet, looking very out of place, keeping their eyes down, not making eye contact with anybody. They sat down hastily on three gilt chairs.

"They'll break those chairs!" Toby warned.

"Watch them." Joseph demanded. "Ibrahim, you follow them everywhere they go. Toby, you'd better go with Ibrahim. Don't let them get to the bear cages. They must not know that we've got their bears here. Don't let them out of your sight."

"But I put three of the bears out in the compound," Ibrahim reminded the others.

"Xin-Hui and Faradilla, as soon as Yusof has finished his speech, you two run over to the bear compound and keep an eye on the three bears out there. Vinod, you keep an eye on all the rest of the creatures. We do not want the Evil Palm Oil Baron to steal any. I just hope they don't leave the marquee before the end of Yusof's speech."

"I do not think they will. The food is too good and it will be served straight after Bapa's finished talking. There will be wine too, and I do not think they will want to miss that." Faradilla smiled shyly.

"Bert, Bert! Get a photo of those three, can you. Oh God, Bert, I hope they are not going to make trouble." Shirley whispered as Bert passed by. Bert gave her the thumbs up and continued snapping as if she had said nothing. But she knew he had heard her.

Mr Brown stood up and tapping the lectern with a small mallet, he cleared his throat. He explained how the charity "The Forest Sanctuary" had been formed and why and how everyone would benefit from it. Then he introduced Yusof.

Yusof made a splendid speech, all about saving the forest and the creatures in it and what a great benefit it was to man to have that forest here in Malagiar. He emphasized that plants were providing spectacular cures for all sorts of ailments. He mentioned Vinca Rosea, used in the treatment of childhood leukaemia, Cinchona – anti-malarial, Casia tora – hypertension and asthma, Achyranthes aspera for heart conditions. The names of the plants were too much for the children to take in or the symptoms they cured but they understood the overall content of his speech. He explained how important it is to live in harmony with nature, side by side with the creatures who do us no harm. And so he went on. But the children were not listening. All their concentration was on Ah Kong, the Fat Superintendent and the Evil Palm Oil Baron. Apart from Vinod, who had seen the Fat Superintendent, they had only seen Ah Kong before and they were fascinated.

Everybody clapped when Yusof had finished speaking. Then Professsor Profundo made a gracious little speech about being allowed to pursue his love of botany in the Malagian forests and the Prime Minister stood up. The children could see the Evil Palm Oil Baron glowering at the Prime Minister but he did not dare raise his head in case he was recognised.

The Prime Minister made a grand speech, telling everyone how wonderful Yusof and Aishah were and what great things they were doing for the preservation of the forest, and

Professor Profundo's work was also absolutely essential to the future wellbeing of the nation.

By then, everybody present had been given either a glass of orange juice or a glass of wine, depending on their preference. The Muslims and Hindi did not drink alcohol and the children were certainly not allowed it. They drank a toast "to the future of the Forest Sanctuary". It was all rather thrilling and for a moment the children forgot the Evil Palm Oil Baron and his henchmen. Then large trays of steaming hot food were brought in to the marquee and placed on the tables. The ladies of the village had provided a feast and everyone tucked in. But the children had no appetite. Too busy watching the Evil Palm Oil Baron, the Fat Superintendent and Ah Kong, they could not eat.

Berminyak, who had loitered close to the kampong for several days, had been particularly interested to see everyone disappearing into the marquee. The village was virtually unoccupied. Taking advantage of the clapping noise, he closed in on a pair of chickens scratching hopefully in the dust. Slowly he approached them. They were too busy to see him until it was too late. Opening his huge jaws wide, the two chickens slithered down almost unnoticed. "Aaagh!" That was better. Now he would find a shady spot to sleep and digest his meal.

"Ah Kong must surely recognise us from the Great Fight" Toby whispered to Joseph.

"I know. That's what worries me."

Shirley Pooper approached them.

"Joseph, you and the children go outside, spread out and keep a look out for all the animals, especially the bears. I have a bad feeling about these people. Bert and I shall watch them here in the marquee but I shall have to keep out of sight. Both Ah Kong and the Evil Palm Oil Baron will recognise me."

Toby hastily whispered in his father, Professor Profundo's ear. The Professor looked up quickly, a surprised expression on his face. He scanned the back of the marquee. Then he spotted them. He recognised Ah Kong and the Evil Palm Oil Baron, and presumed that the fat ugly woman was the Fat Superintendent. He gave no indication that he had seen them but pulled out his handkerchief and blew his nose very heartily. He nodded at Toby.

The children slipped, unnoticed, out of the marquee.

CHAPTER 18

"I think I shall go straight to the bear cages, Toby. I want to be ahead of the Evil Palm Oil Baron, rather than behind him. But you stay behind, and you can watch all three of them." Ibrahim handed Toby a whistle. "If they approach the bear cages, blow this whistle, then I shall know. And, Vinod, you had better have a whistle too. If the girls get into trouble, blow it hard." Ibrahim was determined that the Evil Palm Oil Baron, the Fat Supervisor and Ah Kong should get nowhere near the bear cages. He was not sure how he would prevent them, but he would – somehow!

Xin-Hui, Faradilla and Vinod ran off towards the bear enclosure. Thankfully, Abu, Chio Bu, and Kabus Kelabu were right in the middle of the enclosure, lying down beside the big pool, a long way from the public viewing area.

"Do you think they will recognise them? Even with all their bandages?"

"I do not know. It is difficult to tell. Vinod, you had better go and watch the other creatures. We shall be alright here." Xin-Hui looked up, scanning the trees on the edge of the forest, adjoining the bear enclosure. "Look! There is Tunku – and Puteri, and all the family."

Sure enough, there they were, watching everything with interest. They grinned and waved at the children.

"They will not allow the Evil Palm Oil Baron to get anywhere near the bears." Vinod was greatly relieved. Happier now at leaving the girls alone, he headed off.

Ibrahim sought out his favourite shady spot, and lay down to wait. He could see all the bear cages from here, and look all the way down the path people would follow to get here. These cages were out of bounds to the public, and not part of the Opening Day viewing areas, but Ibrahim wanted to make sure nobody got near the bears. They were still far too traumatized and sick to be introduced to the public. And he certainly did not want the Evil Palm Oil Baron, the Fat Supervisor, or Ah Kong to know the bears were here.

Back in the Marquee, The Evil Palm Oil Baron and Ah Kong had both donned big hats with wide brims which partially hid their faces. They were also wearing sunglasses. The Fat Supervisor made no effort to conceal her identity. She gazed around aggressively, tucking in to huge mountains of food off a plate piled so high Toby thought it would break. *'Can she really eat all that?'* The Evil Palm Oil Baron and Ah Kong shuffled about, keeping their eyes down. They did not eat much, but they downed a few glasses of wine very quickly. Ah Kong nudged the Fat Supervisor, tugged at her sleeve. He wanted to leave the marquee, but she had not finished eating, and had no intention of leaving until her plate was quite clean. A small tussle ensued, but she won.

Ah Kong and the Evil Palm Oil Baron were looking decidedly uncomfortable and impatient. The Evil Palm Oil Baron was especially terrified that the Prime Minister might see him and recognise him. He shuddered as he remembered his last meeting with the Prime Minister. He spoke sharply to the Fat Supervisor who, mouth full, dropped her plate immediately. The three of them made their way out of the marquee as quickly as possible. It was not until they were outside that the Evil Palm Oil Baron breathed a sigh of relief.

"Do you really think these people stole our bears?" The Baron was perspiring copiously. "Yes, Baron, I am sure." The Fat Supervisor nodded her head vigorously. She batted her eyelids at him. Yet again, wearing a tight pink top and too short skirt, she had dressed to kill. Her high heeled shoes were black and shiny. They were rubbing her heels and she was developing great big blisters, but she would not tell the Evil Palm Oil Baron. She was still intent on becoming his wife. She pawed his arm with her stubby fingers, smiling affectionately at him.

"Those children! Those Brats! I recognise them." Ah Kong growled. "They were there, taking part in the Great Fight. And that Mad Professor! He was there, tearing about on an elephant. I would not put anything past them." Ah Kong was terrified of the Evil Palm Oil Baron, and was only too well aware of what punishment he might inflict for losing the bears.

The Evil Palm Oil Baron reflected on the events of the last few days. He recalled how the Fat Supervisor and Ah Kong had stood in front of him, trembling, recounting how all the bears, even old Kulat, had disappeared without trace. He recalled having gone cold, and then hot with rage. He had stamped his feet and shouted abuse at them. He had lashed out at Ah Kong, intending to hit him, but Ah Kong had ducked. They had all piled into the Evil Palm Oil Baron's big black limousine and driven to the bear bile farm. He still could not get over his astonishment at finding absolutely nothing there – apart from a few twisted, rusting old metal cages. No barns, no sheds, nothing! Even the perimeter fence had been flattened.

The Fat Supervisor – mad woman that she was – had insisted the monkeys had something to do with it.

"Monkeys! How could monkeys do this, you stupid woman?" the Evil Palm Oil Baron had shouted at her. "If you do not find out what happened here, I promise you the rest of your life will not be worth living." he had screamed. And then he had kicked her – hard, and pulled her hair.

"If you do not get those bears back, I promise you will be punished." he had screamed at them.

The Fat Supervisor had taken herself off to the market where she heard rumours that things were afoot at Yusof's kampong. She had hung around for a long time, listening to everyone's conversations. She learned that The Forest Sanctuary was soon to open, and that there would be a big opening ceremony. They were building big compounds and cages – expecting an influx of special creatures in the very near future. Nobody had actually said the creatures were bears; she had merely put two and two together and worked it out for herself. Well, she hoped the creatures were bears. (She was very cunning.) Because if they were not, she did not dare to think what the Evil Palm Oil Baron would do to her.

And now, here they were, at the opening of The Forest Sanctuary, and not a bear in sight.

And the Evil Palm Oil Baron seemed particularly disgruntled to find the Prime Minister here. She took a deep breath.

"Let us go this way" she indicated the trail path, keeping her fingers crossed. The three of them trudged off, the Fat Supervisor limping because of her blisters. There were dens in the ground, and platforms in the trees. They saw many creatures, monitor lizards, snakes, pangolins, civet cats, monkeys, birds, but no bears. Finally, they came to the bear compound and there, right in the middle, too far away to get a close look, were three bears. One of them had only one leg. They peered at the bears, uncertain.

"Hello" a little voice said. Faradilla was standing beside them, the baby monkey on her shoulder. "Aren't the bears sweet! But they are wild, and we cannot get near to them. Bapa will return them to the forest as soon as they are better."

"What do you want?"

The Evil Palm Oil Baron huffed and puffed; Ah Kong glowered at her; and the Fat Supervisor looked as if she was about to squash her. Vinod, seeing Faradilla with them, blew his whistle. Toby and Joseph came running.

The Evil Palm Oil Baron, Ah Kong and the Fat Supervisor, seeing the boys running up, turned, and made off in the other direction.

"Whew!" Vinod said.

"They are not very nice people, are they." Faradilla said.

"Watch out! They're heading for the cages." Joseph broke into a run, closely followed by Toby, Vinod, Xin-Hui and Faradilla. Whatever happened, they must not allow these horrible people to get anywhere near the bear cages. Taking a detour, they found Ibrahim.

"They're coming this way." Joseph shouted. "Hurry! We have got to head them off."

The children hurried down the path, away from the cages, anticipating that they would meet the Evil Palm Oil Baron and his cronies en route. Instead, who should come strolling along, deep in conversation, but Professor Profundo and the Prime Minister.

"Why, children, I was just telling the Prime Minister about your amazing feat in rescuing all these bears, and the Prime Minister would really like to see them for himself, wouldn't you, Teo." He turned, smiling, to the Prime Minister.

"Indeed, I would, Professor. And you, children, it seems that you get up to something every school holiday."

"Yes, Prime Minister. Thank you, Prime Minister, but..." Joseph was looking anxiously down the path. *'Where are they. They should be here any minute, and we have got to turn them away.'*

"You look anxious, Joseph." Professor Profundo commented. "Is anything wrong?"
"No, Professor, well, yes." Joseph could not lie.
"What is it?"

"The Evil Palm Oil Baron is here with Ah Kong, and that Fat Supervisor who was at the bear bile farm works for him too, and we think they are trying to find out where the bears are." The words tumbled out.

"The bear bile farm?" the Prime Minister's eyebrows had shot up into his hairline. "My dear child, you must be mistaken. Bear bile farms are banned in Malagiar."

"Yes, Prime Minister. But they were stealing bear cubs from the forest. That's how we found out, and then we found the bile farm, and it was a horrible place, a terrible place. So we decided to rescue the bears, and we brought them all here. The creatures of the forest helped us. And now we think the Evil Palm Oil Baron is going to try and get his bears back. And we do not want them to come anywhere near the bear cages. We do not want them to see the bears, and we do not want the bears to see them. If the bears see the Fat Supervisor or Ah Kong, they will get really distressed."

"They are so afraid, those poor bears. They have been horribly tortured, sometimes for years." Xin-Hui piped up.

"They were in so much pain." Faradilla added.

"They could not even walk" was Vinod's contribution.

"Bapa says they will be traumatised for a very long time. He even had to put some to sleep, they were in such a bad state." Ibrahim added.

"That is true." The children had not noticed Yusof and Shirley Pooper approaching. "Prime Minister, I have something to put to you." Yusof continued. "Shirley Pooper here has written an article for the South East Asia Gazette about the rescue of these bears, but her editor will not allow it to go to print because he feels the bears are stolen property. He believes the children stole them from whoever owned the bear bile farm, and we now believe that person is the Evil Palm Oil Baron. If the children have, indeed, stolen the bears, they will have to be returned."

"Oh no!"

"Bapa, you cannot." "They cannot go back." "That would be too cruel."

The children all cried out at once. The Prime Minister looked around at their faces, and smiled.

"But, Yusof, I understand these bears were stolen from the forest in the first place. Have I not placed a protection order on the forest?

Nobody is allowed to take creatures from the forest. That, after all, is stealing."

"Yes, Prime Minister, and the cubs were only taken recently. They have, incidentally, all been returned to the forest where they belong. But most of these bears were removed from the forest many years before you placed that protection order on it."

"Then, my dear Yusof, I shall have to make that protection order retrospective. I shall do so immediately, I assure you."

"You mean the bears will not be considered stolen?" Shirley Pooper was very relieved.

"That is exactly what I mean. The Evil Palm Oil Baron had no right to have those bears in the first place, Shirley."

"Oh, Prime Minister, thank-you. Thank-you!" Shirley rushed off to telephone Sam, the editor, and tell him, so that her article could go to press the next day.

"And now, if you will excuse me, Prime Minister, I have something important to do." Yusof, bowing slightly, left them. By now, members of the public were swarming all over the Sanctuary. He was pleased to see so many there. He called over some of the biggest and strongest men in the village, and they went off in search of the Evil Palm Oil Baron, Ah Kong, and the Fat Supervisor.

They found the Evil Palm Oil Baron, Ah Kong and the Fat Supervisor lurking behind a big bougainvillia bush. They were rounded up by the village men and marched off the premises. The Evil Palm Oil Baron was furious. Flouted again! Ah Kong shuffled along, and the Fat Supervisor flounced.

"Please do not come back again. You will not be welcome here." Yusof told them.

A little later, the Prime Minister took his leave. He had enjoyed himself at The Forest Sanctuary. He was particularly fond of Professor Profundo, and of Yusof, but he was beginning to regard the children with considerable affection as well. They made him feel young again.

Finally, everyone had gone, even Shirley Pooper and Bert. The opening of The Forest Sanctuary had been a great success, and Shirley's whole article was to go into the South East Asia Gazette tomorrow. She needed to get back to the office, to add the final touches.

CHAPTER 19

The following morning, the children had a lie-in. They were very tired. After breakfast they strolled down to the Sanctuary, chattering as they went, about the previous day's excitement.

"It's good that the Prime Minister said the Evil Palm Oil Baron can't own the bears." Toby said. "I wonder what made him start the bear thing. After all, he grows palm oil plantations."

"But don't forget that the Prime Minister banned him from having any more plantations. I think he had tried to bribe the government, or something. But he was sent to prison and I think his plantations were confiscated, so he probably thought this was a way to make some money. My Dad says he's a nasty piece of work." Joseph said.

"So – I suppose he's got out now."

"He must have done. I don't like him at all. I'm just glad he's not coming back here again." Xin-Hui shivered as she thought of the Evil Palm Oil Baron. "Ooh, do you think he escaped?"

"Don't be silly." Vinod chipped in "Do not forget to get today's papers. Shirley Pooper's article is going in today, and we are in it."

Faradilla's eyes opened wide "Will there be more photographs of us? And the bears?" "I expect so. Bert was running around taking photos all the time."

They quickened their pace. "Come on. Let's get the chores done. Then we can go and find a newspaper." Ibrahim broke into a gentle trot. The others followed.

A few hours later, the children were gathered round a crisp and clean brand new newspaper spread out on a big table. Shirley Pooper had done justice to the bear rescue. Her story missed nothing. Bert's photographs were harrowing.

"Those poor bears. I'm so glad we rescued them. Oh, and look! There's poor old Kulat. I hope he is in heaven now." Faradilla was close to tears as she remembered the events of that extraordinary evening. "And there's Cahaya

Bulan with little Guruh, and she's carrying some of the bears."

"There are the baby bears, running in the forest. They are so naughty!" Xin-Hui giggled. The boys were reading through Shirley's article very carefully. She had got nothing wrong, faithfully reporting all the events of the evening when they rescued the bears.

Aishah joined the children. "Well," she sighed "I suppose this means we are going to have reporters all over the kampong again. I just hope they do not trample on my plants."

"No, Mama, they will come to see the bears." Ibrahim said. "I do not think you will have to worry."

"Can the bears be put out in the compound yet?"

"Not really. Well, there are three out there, but the rest cannot go out yet. They are still not well enough. And if they want to see the cubs ... well, that is just too bad." Ibrahim smiled. He was glad the bear cubs would not be exposed to all those reporters poking and prying and flashing cameras. "I wonder how they are getting on. Has anyone seen Hitam Malam?" he looked around, but the others shook their heads.

Faradilla was playing with the little monkey. Aishah spoke to her, quite sternly.

"Faradilla, you must find that baby's Mummy. Bapa will be very cross with you if you do not."

Faradilla looked suitably crestfallen. "Yes, Mama." She wandered off.

~

For several days, Yusof had spent as much spare time as he could in the woodshed, carving, whittling, and whistling as he worked. He would allow nobody to enter, and said what he was working on was secret, an experiment. Not even Aishah was allowed to visit him there.

The world, it seemed, was full of secrets. Ibrahim saw Number One Son in the forest one day

"Number One Son" he called "What are you up to?" Number One Son just shrugged and grinned.

"Busy!" he said, and headed off.

Professor Profundo was working in the Sanctuary laboratory. He was in his element, but very secretive about his "research".

~

'If we are going to have lots of Reporters coming here, there will not be so much time left for secrets.' Ibrahim, who did not like being left out, was consoled by the thought.

"Ah, you have found the newspaper." Yusof was smiling broadly at the children. He was joined by Professor Profundo.

"I say, Shirley Pooper has done a splendid job, a splendid job! She's done us proud." He was beaming. "She says here we're all heroes. Oh I say!" Professor Profundo was lost for words.

"Look, there's a photo of me carrying a cub" Toby said. He was very pleased. The photograph made him look quite handsome. "And look at that one of Matahari and the other elephants with all the bears. And there's Rambut Sutera and the Head man."

"I do not think they will be too happy about that. They do not like having their photographs taken."

"Why not?"

"Something about the photograph taking away their spirit. I am not sure."

"Now, children, you know from your last adventure, that it is best to say as little as possible to the reporters if they start asking questions, and I am sure they will." Yusof looked towards the entrance of the Sanctuary. There were already lines of people queuing up to get in, several of them looked suspiciously like reporters.

"I think we might go into the forest this afternoon, Bapa, and collect some herbs." Ibrahim intended to avoid any reporters as much as possible. Being a hero was really very embarrassing.

"That might be sensible." Yusof agreed.

Slipping round the back of the kampong, so as not to be seen, the children were soon engulfed within the forest. Each carried a basket and a small knife. Yusof needed more healing herbs. Ibrahim and Faradilla knew which herbs to look for and where they were. Engrossed in what they were doing, they did not see Number One Son until he jumped down beside them.

"Oh, Number One Son, you gave us a fright. It is so nice to see you again. But where is Tunku?" Ibrahim asked.

Number One Son told Ibrahim that Tunku was busy; he was rounding up all the important creatures for Number One Son's Naming Day, which would be tomorrow. The children, Yusof, and Professor Profundo were invited. They were to come to the glade tomorrow at the time of the mid-day sun.

The children were very excited to receive the invitation.

"Oh Goodness me!" cried Vinod. "What a great holiday this is!"

"Will Cahaya Bulan be there, with little Guruh?" Xin-Hui asked immediately.

"Perhaps I had better take the little monkey with me, and then I can ask about his Mummy." Faradilla suggested.

"Yes, Faradilla, that is a good idea. Oh gosh, this is great!" Joseph was as excited as anyone. Toby did a little dance. "Yes, yes, yes!" He punched the air.

Number One Son's Naming Day was something special; the children were determined not to miss it.

Ibrahim responded gravely to Number One Son, telling him that they would all be there tomorrow, and Number One Son left them. There was still a lot to do.

CHAPTER 20

The next day, everyone was up at daybreak, and chores got done in no time. Faradilla, Xin- Hui and Vinod were particularly anxious to be off. They had only once been allowed to go to the glade before, and that was when they had gone with Yusof to heal the creatures who had retreated there after the great fight. It was the animals' special place. Finally, everyone was ready to set off. Even Aishah had agreed to come. She and Yusof had a particular relationship with Tunku, and were delighted that his Number One Son should be having his Naming Day, able to take over some of the responsibilities which now lay heavily on old Tunku's shoulders.

Faradilla was carrying the baby monkey. It snuggled up to her. She had bravely told it she was going to try and find it's Mummy, who would surely be at the gathering for Number One Son's Naming Day.

As they walked through the forest Yusof explained to Professor Profundo and the children that Tunku was particularly precious to them. It was a long story.

Tunku had been a baby orang-utan in the jungle, learning from his Mummy, just like any other baby orang-utan when, one day, some bad men came and shot his Mummy, and took Tunku away in a small wooden cage. Tunku was just three years old, and the bullet which killed his Mummy had grazed the side of Tunku's head, leaving a wound which would eventually become a big scar. Orang-utans need and depend on their Mummies for at least seven years, Yusof explained. Yusof's father, who was a Bomoh, had found the body of Tunku's Mummy. He recognised her, and knew that her son was missing. He determined to find the little fellow.

"What's a Bomoh?"

"A Bomoh is a traditional healer, he works with herbs. It is from my father that I learned so much. I was just a young boy then".

Yusof's father had searched and searched in the forest, but could not find the baby orang- utan. The Orang-Asli had helped him, but they could not find it either. Then Yusof's father decided to look in the markets. Someone must have taken the baby to sell. Trafficking in wild animals, although illegal, was very profitable.

It had taken Yusof's father three weeks, trekking around the local markets, taking Yusof with him, asking lots of questions, before they found the little orang-utan, still in the same tiny wooden cage. The baby was badly traumatised, in shock. It was being sold at one of the markets.

Yusof's father had bartered for a long time with the man selling the baby orang-utan. Finally, after Yusof's father had threatened to report him to the police, the man sold the baby to him. The wound on its head had gone septic, and the poor baby was desperately thin. They took it back to the kampong, where they nursed it for several days until it got a little better.

"It was a pathetic little thing, just sitting and staring into space, but gradually it put on weight and gathered strength. We were beginning to realize, though, just what a bright little thing it was. I spent hours playing with it." Yusof smiled to himself at his memories.

Yusof's father had made a big cage for the baby. It even had its own little cot and toys in there. One night the baby orang-utan had managed to unlock the cage and escape. It fled into the forest.

"At just three years old, it did not stand a chance alone in the forest. We looked and looked for it, but never found it." Yusof said. "Until finally we gave up, thinking it must surely have died."

"Then, twenty years later, a huge glossy, well-muscled male orang-utan turned up at the kampong. He was very wary of people and would let nobody near him, but he hung around. As long as we did not approach him, he was fine. He seemed to enjoy watching us. I could not understand why the orang-utan was there, what he wanted. Ibrahim was just a baby, a toddler. One day, Ibrahim disappeared. Aishah found him snuggling up to that great strong orang-utan. It had Ibrahim wrapped in it's arms. We were very frightened, I can tell you, but that great big male was so gentle with Ibrahim, it was incredible. Then I spotted, under the hair, a long scar across the side of his head. Gradually, it dawned on me that this must be the little orang-utan we had tried to rescue all those years ago. He had come back. I do not know how he managed to survive in the forest alone. He must have found a foster-mother somewhere.

We noticed that he was very aggressive towards all the other orang-utans which visited the kampong. He was not aggressive towards us, but very wary. There were fights, big fights, with other males, but this orang-utan always won. It was obvious he had become the dominant male of the forest. So we called him Tunku, a fitting name, don't you think?"

"So, the little baby you tried to rescue all those years ago came back?"

"Yes, that's right. And he developed a very special relationship with Ibrahim. Ibrahim could play with him for hours. He tumbled all over him, pulling his hair, demanding piggy-back rides, and Tunku never once complained or displayed any degree of intolerance.

Then, just as he had come, Tunku disappeared. But he returned after a month or so, and this time he had with him a pretty little female orang-utang, and she had a baby. It is almost as if he wanted to show his family off, maybe even to get our approval. They were inseparable. He still allowed Ibrahim to play with him, but the little female and the baby were always by his side. We called her Puteri and, well, you know the rest. Ibrahim and Number One Son grew up together, and Tunku is now the undisputed Lord of the Canopies."

"So, let me see, that makes Tunku in his mid thirties." Professor Profundo was amazed at Yusof's story.

"Yes, Professor. That is a good age for a creature of the forest, and Tunku is still fit, but I worry about him. The great fight took more out of him that he realises. And he is still wary of humans. So I am especially pleased that he is now handing over some of his responsibilities to Number One Son."

"But he trusts you and Aishah. I've seen how he reacts to you." Yusof smiled. "Yes, I believe he does."

The glade was already filling up with creatures. Matahari and his tribe were all there, Cahaya Bulan keeping Guruh close by her side. The monkeys and apes were there, the cats, the squirrels, the pangolins, the forest rhino, the tigers, and the bear, even some crocodiles from the swamps. Hitam Malam was there with Hantu, and all the little cubs were there with their Mummies and foster Mummies. It seemed that the whole of the Orang Asli tribe were there–even the children. They were led by the Head man.

"Ooh look, lah!" Faradilla squealed in excitement. "There is Cahaya Bulan with little Guruh".

Vinod ran up to one of the bear cubs, giving it a big squeezy hug. The cub sneezed.

Yusof lifted Faradilla, Xin-Hui and Vinod up into the branches of a tree.

"Shin up, boys" he instructed the others. "You will get a better view from up there." He lifted Aishah up, and started to climb up himself, closely followed by Professor Profundo who huffed and puffed a lot, but made it up into the tree.

"We've got a really good viewing platform up here." The Professor's enthusiasm was undiminished.

"Faradilla, I have asked Tunku to make an announcement about that baby monkey. You absolutely must give it back to its Mummy. She is bound to be here." Yusof was stern. His daughter was too inclined to get attached to animals which did not belong to her. Aishah smiled gently at Faradilla and gave her a big hug.

"You know it is for the best, Faradilla." she said. Faradilla hugged the baby monkey.

The glade quickly filled up. The creatures were shoving and jostling each other, all anxious to get the best view. Tunku, Puteri and Number One Son were on the hillock, slightly raised above everyone else, where they could be seen. Number One Son was flanked by Tunku on one side, and Puteri on the other. Faradilla, Xin-Hui, Vinod and Toby were entranced. They had only ever been to the glade once before, when they helped dress the wounds of the creatures after the Great Fight. It was, after all, a special privilege to be here.

"Look! Look! There is Hitam Malam. He has got Hantu and some of the cubs with him." Xin-Hui shrieked.

All heads swivelled. They watched the little cubs for a while. They were very happy, gambolling along beside Hitam Malam and Hantu, who guarded them jealously. Their Mummies were there too. Nobody would ever again be able to take cubs away from this forest.

Standing upright, Tunku held up his long arm for silence. All the noise and the jostling stopped. He had their full attention.

"My friends, I have reigned as Lord of the Canopies for many years now. I hope I have performed well *(everyone cheers, rumbles, snorts, hoots, or whatever they do)*. But now I feel I am becoming old. It is time for Number One Son to take over the greater part of my responsibilities. I believe I have trained him well, and he will be a worthy and undisputed Lord of the Canopies. He is my son, but he has also fought many battles to earn his place."

"Fought many battles! What does he mean?" whispered Xin-Hui. "Sshh, I shall tell you later." Faradilla put her finger to her lips.

He took Number One Son's hand and, holding it aloft, he proclaimed

"I honour you, my son, with the name 'Tuhan'. Henceforth you will be known as Tuhan, Lord of the Canopies. May you live up to your name, and protect the forest and its creatures from any ills which may occur."

Number One Son, now to be called Tuhan, rose up himself.

"I thank you, My Father, for all that you have taught me, and given to me. I shall do my best to emulate you and to honour you, to be a worthy Lord of the Canopies, and protect the forest and all within it." *(More cheers, rumbles, snorts, hoots, grunts, and so on, and lots of stamping in approval.)*

Tunku waited for everyone to calm down, and raised his hand to make one more announcement:

"There is a human child here who has a very big heart and who kindly rescued a baby monkey which lost his Mummy. She found the baby, or maybe the baby found her, in the silent part of the forest. If the Mummy is here, please can you come forward, and claim your infant."

All the creatures were looking around them when, out of the trees, dropped a young female Macaque. She was chittering excitedly. Cahaya Bulan lifted Faradilla out of the tree in which she was sitting, and bore her over to the hillock. She lowered her gently to the ground. The baby monkey was in Faradilla's arms. But, as soon as it saw its Mummy, it started chittering and chattering in great agitation. Faradilla put the baby down, and it leapt into its mother's arms, clinging to her for dear life. *(cheers, rumbles, snorts, hoots, grunts, and stamping of feet)*. Faradilla, abashed, did not know what to do with herself. She was rescued by Cahaya Bulan, who lifted her up and carried her back to the tree where the others were waiting for her.

The creatures on the floor of the glade, the birds and monkeys in the trees, who had all maintained a respectful silence throughout Tunku's speech, and then Tuhan's speech, now raised their voices in unison, singing a hymn of the forest. It was an ancient hymn, as old as time itself, and sent shivers of delight through the children who heard it.

Puteri was beaming from ear to ear. She had one arm draped around Tunku, and the other draped around Tuhan. Number Two Son sat quietly on her lap. Yusof indicated that it was time to leave. He lifted Faradilla, Xin-Hui, Aishah, and Vinod down. Ibrahim, Joseph, Toby and Professor Profundo could fend for themselves. They were all very quiet on the way home, remembering all they had seen, thinking. Yusof interrupted their thoughts:

"Children, I cannot emphasise too heavily that you must NEVER, NEVER tell anyone what you have seen today, or where. We were very privileged to have been allowed into the glade, and I do not want any one of us to abuse that privilege. You must keep this experience a secret for ever."

The children all nodded heartily in agreement. *'Oh Dear! Another secret!'* thought Ibrahim. "Will we still be able to play with

Number One S..., I mean Tuhan, Bapa?"
Faradilla asked Yusof.

"Of course you can, Faradilla, but he will
be a lot busier now, and will have less time
for play."

Xin-Hui nudged Faradilla.

"What did Tunku mean when he said
Number One Son had fought many battles?"
"Well. I think they have to prove they are
worthy of becoming Lord of the Canopies by
fighting off all the other male orang-utans who
would also like to be Lord of the Canopies."

CHAPTER 21

The Forest Sanctuary had fallen into a kind of routine. The children arrived in the morning, not too early. They helped change the bedding of the animals there, changed feeding bowls and water bowls. Occasionally they were allowed to brush the bears, but not often. Yusof had told them to leave the bears alone as much as possible. The bears still had a long way to go before they could begin to trust humans, or adjust to any life other than being cooped up in tiny cages.

Yusof did his veterinary rounds in the middle of the morning. A resident veterinary surgeon was no longer needed; the bears were recovering nicely from their wounds and sores. The other creatures occasionally needed a dressing, or medicine, but none of them was any longer seriously ill. Most of the residents at the Sanctuary, however, were wounded or maimed in some way, and therefore unable to return to the forest.

Abu, Chio Bu, and Kabus Kelabu went into the big compound each morning, and there enjoyed the water pool, and the sunshine. Although he had a leg amputated, Abu was getting about very well. He was even beginning to climb a little. All three bears were gaining in strength.

The public were allowed in at 11.00 a.m. each morning, and there was a steady stream, which pleased Yusof, because they paid to come in, and that money helped feed the creatures and pay for their medical needs. He was employing some of the villagers now, to help him, and so he was providing gainful employment, which gave him a nice warm feeling.

Reporters were becoming a nuisance after Shirley Pooper's article had been published, and so, having conferred with the children and Professor Profundo, Yusof agreed that they would give an official Press Interview. The Interview was to be in a couple of days' time, in the Education Hall at the Sanctuary (this is what they had decided to call the classroom; it sounded much more grand than 'classroom'). It was where schoolchildren were given talks about the preservation of the forest. The talks were very popular. Aishah gave the talks, and made them lots of fun.

After his morning rounds, Yusof made for his shed where he was still working secretly. He had been joined there by one of the village men who, Ibrahim told the others, was the best carpenter in the village. Something was going on. But what?

"What if the Evil Palm Oil Baron comes back, or that Fat Supervisor or Ah Kong?" Vinod asked one day. He shivered. Those people really scared him.

"I do not think they will dare. Not after meeting the Prime Minister here. That must have been a shock for them". Joseph chuckled.

"And everybody knows to watch out for them." Ibrahim added.

"They don't give up easily. I suppose they could come back. But what can they do? They can try to steal the bears. They only way they could do that would be to come in the night, and then they would be caught because the village dogs would set up such a noise, and now that Aishah's bought those geese, they do not stand a chance. Geese are the best watchdogs of all." Toby was quite proud that he knew about geese.

"Has anyone seen that snake, Berminyak, lately? Only, a lot of chickens are disappearing from the village. The women are getting very cross. They think a snake is taking them, and I bet it is Berminyak."

"I suppose he can have one or two chickens. After all, without his help we would probably not have rescued the bears."

"But he is taking a lot. He must go back to the forest, and live there. It is too easy for him here. Bapa would be very cross." Faradilla was firm.

"You are right, but how do we get rid of him, lah? He frightens me. He is so big and scary, and he looks all slithery and slimy."

"He is not slithery and slimy. He is very smooth." Vinod said importantly. He had actually stroked Berminyak's skin. He had secretly reached out and touched him in the forest when nobody was looking, because he was so scared of the snake that he thought if he touched it, it might not be so scary.

"I know that, but he looks slithery and slimy." Xin-Hui was indignant.

"We have to tell him." Faradilla said, jumping up. "Let us go now and find him."

"No, Faradilla, Tunku and Matahari are the Lords of the forest. One of them will have to tell him." Ibrahim was right.

"But it is not Tunku any more. It is Tuhan now." "Well, Tuhan then."

Ibrahim went off into the forest. He was going to try and find Tuhan, and ask him to tell Berminyak that he must leave the village chickens alone. If he did not, the villagers would eventually kill him.

"Tuhan, Tuhan, Number One Son." he called. He was finding it difficult to adjust to Tuhan's new name. He heard the monkeys chittering and flying through the branches overhead. They would find Tuhan for him. Sure enough, Tuhan was there within minutes. Grinning, he jumped down beside Ibrahim, and gave him a hug.

Ibrahim explained the villagers' problem with disappearing chickens, and told Tuhan that they suspected Berminyak was the culprit. Tuhan said he would tell Berminyak to leave the village alone. He also said that Tunku was enjoying his retirement from duty, and was deep in the forest with Puteri and Number Two Son.

"Thank you, Tuhan. I shall tell my father. He will be glad to hear your news."

Ibrahim returned to the Sanctuary. "Do not worry about Berminyak. Tuhan will order him back to the forest, and he dare not disobey Tuhan's order. Do not say anything to the villagers. It is best that they do not know. No more chickens will disappear."

The children agreed.

Abu, in the bear compound, got up and hobbled slowly over to the edge of the compound, by the forest. The children watched him. It was unusual for Abu to walk so far in one go. Then they saw, at the edge of the forest, waiting for Abu, Hitam Malam.

"Oh look. He has come to visit Abu." breathed Faradilla. "How sweet."

Yusof had insisted that the compound be accessible to the forest, and so Hitam Malam was able to enter the compound easily. He and Abu lay down together and rolled in the dust together. The children laughed. Hitam Malam spent the whole day in the compound with Abu. Visitors to the Sanctuary did not realise that another bear had entered the compound straight out of the forest, and that the bears could come and go as they pleased.

CHAPTER 22

Yusof and the carpenter were working away in their shed. Nobody knew what they were doing., but there were lots of sounds of sawing, planing, drilling, and chiselling. Then, one day, Yusof emerged with a strange looking contraption made of wood and springs, and leather straps. He went into the bear compound and approached Abu. Abu, knowing this man had helped to heal him, waited quietly. He was no longer afraid. Kneeling by Abu, Yusof strapped the contraption on to him. He concentrated hard, testing the straps, running his fingers down and around them. Suddenly Toby realised what he was doing. "He's giving Abu a false leg." he shouted.

Sure enough, Yusof stood back, and Abu, standing, wobbled. Yusof waited anxiously beside him. After a few seconds, he took a tentative step forward, then another, and another. He seemed to be moving more easily already.

"I say, Yusof, that thing seems to be working. What a jolly idea!" Professor Profundo was impressed.

"If it works well, and improves their quality of life, I shall make them for all the amputees." Yusof answered. Then he said to Ibrahim "Would you go into the forest and find Hitam Malam and Hantu? I think they might like to be here this evening."

"What is happening this evening, Bapa?"

"Wait and see." Yusof went off, heading for his office. There, unbeknown to the children, he telephoned Shirley Pooper, and several of the reporters who had been ferreting around the village for the past several days.

All the children elected to go with Ibrahim into the forest. They loved it, and were no longer afraid of anything there.

"I would rather face Berminyak in the forest than the Evil Palm Oil Baron in the kampong" Vinod said.

"Hitam Malam could be anywhere" Joseph, always the worrier, said.

"He will have stayed within a short distance. He wants to spend time with Abu. I wonder what he will make of Abu's new leg."

"Will Abu be able to go into the forest with Hitam Malam now?"

"Why not? If he wants to, and if he's comfortable, he can go for walks and all that, but he won't be able to live in the forest and fend for himself. He will always need us to look after him."

"Yes. We need to look after all the bears." Faradilla was right.

They spread out, each of the boys taking a different trail, the girls choosing to stay together.

The forest was dry now, the rainy season was over. The pathway underfoot was soft crumbly earth, actually thousands of decayed leaves which had fallen over the years, stifling any sound of their tread as they went. Periodically they called out "Hitam Malam! Hantu!" High overhead, the trees rustled and swayed gently.

"I do love those sounds, of the monkeys, and the birds, and even the cicadas" Xin-Hui told Faradilla. "I used to be so frightened of the forest, and I still hate some of the insects (not all of them), but I especially hate the leeches."

"Leeches are not really bad. They are very helpful for healing, Bapa says."

"I think they are horrible." Xin-Hui shuddered.

At that moment a man stepped onto the trail ahead of them. They gasped. "It is alright, Xin-Hui. It is Rambut Sutera."

"I know. But he is still so scary."

Rambut Sutera smiled at them, but, to Xin-Hui, he looked fiercer than ever. "What are you girls doing here, on your own?"

"We are not alone. They boys are here, too. We are looking for Hitam Malam and Hantu. Bapa wants them to come to the kampong this evening." Faradilla found her voice.

"Ah!" Raising his head, Rambut Sutera let out a long, low cry. It was not particularly loud, but carried a long way. The boys, hearing it and thinking something was wrong, came running as fast as they could.

"What's the matter? What's wrong?"

"Nothing. Rambut Sutera just called Hitam Malam." Xin-Hui was thinking that when she grew up, she might not marry Ibrahim after all; Rambut Sutera would make a very fine husband.

"Hi, Rambut Sutera. We're looking for Hitam Malam. Bapa wants him to come to the compound this evening." Ibrahim grinned cheekily at Rambut Sutera.

"I have already called him. He will be here very soon."

"Oh, thank you. You have saved us a lot of trouble."

Rambut Sutera laughed. His laughter was deep-throated and rich.

"Just as I saved you getting fresh water and brought you mangoes to eat when you were in the forest."

"That was you? Why did you not let us know you were there?" Ibrahim was incredulous. "I could not stay. I was hunting."

"What were you hunting?"

"Pig. Wild pig."

"Did you get it?"

"Yes. Of course. It fed the whole village. We had a big feast." Rambut Sutera laughed again, and Xin-Hui looked at him with renewed respect. "Now I must go. I shall see you this evening." he said mysteriously. And he was gone.

The children sat down to wait for Hitam Malam.

"If Rambut Sutera says he will come, he will come."

"What makes you so sure, Ibrahim?"

"He is the headman's first born son. He will be head man one day, and so his word is his bond. It is sacred."

"The headman's son?" "Yes."

'Then I shall certainly think about marrying him.' Xin-Hui was very impressed.

They heard a soft rustling along the trail and shortly Hitam Malam emerged, followed by Hantu.

Xin-Hui gave him a hug. After all, he had once rescued her from a bear pit.

Ibrahim gave the bears his father's message, and they happily accepted his invitation, but wondered what he wanted to see them for. Ibrahim could not tell them.

CHAPTER 23

Back at the kampong, it seemed the whole village had turned out and were particularly busy working on the padang. They had laid out tables, garlanded with flowers and vines. Lanterns were in the trees, all ready to be lit, and women everywhere were busily cooking. Delicious smells emanated from every house. Nobody had time to talk to the children, tell them what was happening. They were sent down to The Sanctuary where they were told to help with the bears, who were all going to go out into the compound this afternoon, for the first time. "All the bears? Every one of them?"

"Yes, I think they are ready." Yusof said. "They will not really start to heal and live normal lives, or as normal as possible, until we get them out of those cages."

The children ran off to the Sanctuary. This was exciting. A run had been created from the bear cages to the compound. So, when the hatches were opened, the bears could walk down of their own accord, but they would still be frightened, and would need a lot of encouragement.

The hatches were opened. The bears, at first, refused to move. But Abu, Chio Bu and Kabus Kelabu were waiting for them at the other end, snorting and snuffling, giving them encouragement. Chio Bu even came up the runway from the compound end, encouraging the bears to follow her down. Slowly, very slowly, they started to leave their cages. Tentatively, they walked down the runway, stopping, sniffing the air, then slowly continuing.

"They are like cats." Faradilla said "Checking everything." "Wouldn't you, after all they've been through?" Joseph asked her.

It took over an hour, but finally, all the bears had come down into the compound. They could hardly remember grass. They dabbed at it with their paws; they sniffed the air; some of the bolder bears even rolled in the grass. A couple dabbed at the water in the pond. The amputees were managing to walk, but with difficulty. Abu was getting about really well with his false leg.

"Look at them. They are really happy." Xin-Hui squealed.

Vinod counted carefully "Thirty-four bears. That's a lot of bears."

"And we managed to save them all." Joseph was rightly proud of their achievement.

"I am so glad I've been able to see them out in the compound before I go." Toby and Professor Profundo were to return to England the following day. The holiday was nearly over, and he had to get back in time for school.

"England is going to be so dull. Every time I come here, we have a great adventure." Toby was wistful.

"Well, you'll just have to come back next holiday, won't you. Come on, Toby, cheer up." Joseph laughed.

"We shall always be here, Toby, and you can come any time. We want you to come." Ibrahim was serious.

Vinod patted Toby on the back. "Come on, Toby, cheer up." he said.

Yusof approached them. He had been watching with satisfaction as the bears emerged from their cages. They had made great progress.

"Now, children, you are to go and clean yourselves up. Remember that I have invited the Press to come this evening, and they will want to question you. Do not look so worried. Your parents will be coming, Aishah and I will be there, and the Professor, and we shall help you. And, I have got a surprise for you as well." He grinned mysteriously.

"Oh, we had forgotten about the reporters."

'What is going on? More secrets'.

Wanting to spend as little time as possible away from the bears, the children rushed off to clean themselves up.

When they returned, there were already queues of reporters at the Sanctuary gate. Aishah let them in and ushered them to the Education Hall. The parents arrived, and Shirley Pooper and Bert. The head man and Rambut Sutera arrived, but they did not go in to the Education Hall. They stayed outside, near the bear compound, where they were delighted to see all the bears. Hitam Malam and Hantu arrived, and quietly, unnoticed, joined the bears in the compound.

"Now, children" Yusof called "Everyone is waiting for you. I shall talk to the reporters, and they will ask you some questions, but not too many. You must be getting used to this by now."

He tried to reassure them, but it was a nerve-wracking business, all this publicity stuff. The children trooped in to the Education Hall, and made their way to the small dais at the front, where Yusof had placed chairs for them. He came in with them, and made a speech.

"Ladies and gentlemen, welcome to the Forest Sanctuary. As you know, we have already had an official opening here, and the story about these children and the way they rescued bears from an evil bear bile farm is already history. However, you have been invited here for a specific reason.

These children rescued thirty-nine adult bears and twenty cubs. One old bear, Kulat, was too sick to be rescued, but you all know his story. Thanks to Shirley Pooper, it was reported in the South East Asia Gazette. I believe that, in time, Kulat will become a legend. Due to the appalling practice of bear bile farming, I have had to put five bears to sleep, as they were in great pain and would not have survived, and we now have fifteen amputees among the bears. Many have had to have their gall bladders removed because of infections. I am happy to say that all surviving bears are doing well.

The twenty cubs have been returned to the forest, adopted by adult bears. That is absolutely the right thing for them.

You are invited here today because the children want you to be aware of just how evil and unnecessary this terrible practice is - of milking bile from bears. What little benefit the bile provides can easily be gained from natural resources such as herbs. Here, at the Forest Sanctuary, we are dedicated to eradicating this vile practice. It is already unlawful here, in Malagiar, but there are those who still operate secret bear bile farms. They MUST be stopped.

At this Sanctuary, we shall take in any bear in need. If you hear of any such bear bile farms, therefore, please inform us.

If you have questions to ask of the children, please ask them, and then we shall proceed to the bear compound, where I have something to show you. Ladies and Gentlemen, thank you." And he finished. Everybody clapped.

Several reporters put their hand up. Yusof pointed to one.

"A question for the children. Why do you do it? Why are you so concerned with the preservation of the forest, rescuing bears, and all the rest of it?"

As the eldest, Joseph stood up and came to the front of the dais.

"We did not set out to do these things. They just happened, really. But we all believe that we should live in harmony with nature. Why do we have to destroy it? What benefit do we get from that?" He sat down abruptly.

Ibrahim stood up.

"The forest and the creatures in it have so much to give us, but we humans are too busy being greedy to appreciate it."

"Yes, and I live in a high-rise apartment, lah, and there is concrete everywhere. It's hard and dull and hurts when I fall, but in the forest it is green and soft, and I am not afraid there any more."

The reporters asked more questions, and the children answered as best they could until, finally, Yusof said

"I think that is enough questions now. If you would like to follow me, ladies and gentlemen." And he led the way out of the door and down to the bear compound. There was something in the middle, big and covered up with canvas.

"Ladies and gentlemen, there are thirty-four bears in this compound. Most of them came out for the first time today, so please do not frighten them. They are still very fragile."

Entering the compound, he called the head man of the Orang Asli to his side.

"I have invited the Head Man of the Orang Asli, conservators of the forest, to unveil this memorial to one of the bravest and most badly treated bears I have ever heard of. In his honour, this compound will henceforth be known as The Kulat Enclosure."

And the head man pulled off the canvas covering to reveal a huge statue of Kulat, standing over six feet high, carved out of teak. It was magnificent. The children gasped. Bert was busy taking photographs.

"Oh My!" Professor Profundo was greatly moved.

"Who carved that statue? It is magnificent." One of the reporters asked.

Yusof beckoned the carpenter who had been working secretly in the shed for the past few days. He came forward sheepishly. Everybody clapped.

'Aah, so that was the secret! And then there was Abu's false leg. Perhaps secrets are not so bad after all.'

One of the reporters, addressing Yusof, said

"You said, sir, that there are thirty-four bears in the compound, but I have just counted thirty- six."

"My dear young man, you must be mistaken."

Shirley Pooper had spotted Hitam Malam and Hantu, and, followed by Bert, made her way over to them.

"Bert, can you get a picture of the wild bears with the captive ones?" "Of course I can."

The reporter who had counted thirty-six bears joined them. "There are thirty-six bears here, not thirty-four." he said.

"You must be mistaken." Shirley said, looking directly at Hitam Malam. "There are thirty- four rescued bears.

The bears in what was now to be known as the Kulat Enclosure were a little wary of all these people, and kept their distance; they had plenty of room to get away. The amputees were getting about, much to Yusof's delight, but slowly. Abu, however, with his false leg, was racing around.

Shirley Pooper spotted Abu's false leg, and asked Yusof about it.

"Yes. It is an experiment. If it works, I shall make legs for all the amputees."

"It certainly seems to be working right now, Yusof. Well done." she said enthusiastically. Aishah announced that food and drink were available on the padang, and the reporters, always ready for a good scoff, rushed off. The children were left behind to help put the bears back to bed in their cages, where they would be safe for the night. Hitam Malam and Hantu lay down in the enclosure to sleep.

By time the children got to the padang, everyone was eating and chatting merrily. And there was still plenty of food left for them: mee goring, nasi goring, kway teow, murtabak, pak- choi in oyster sauce, satay, rice, rendang, sambal prawns, and freshly baked roti, lots of fresh fruit, and plenty to drink. It was another really good party. Tunku, Puteri and Tuhan were there with Number Two Son, and lots of monkeys and gibbons, watching from the trees. Mr and Mrs Smith were chatting to Aishah, Mrs Singh dandled Vinod's little brother on her knee, and Mr and Mrs Chan chatted happily to Professor Profundo.

Katak, the dog, who was always at Faradilla's side, was having a lovely time. He was fed so many titbits that his little tummy was quite full, and he felt very sleepy. Even Berminyak, banished from the kampong by Tuhan, was lurking on the edge of the padang. He might just get a tasty chicken when nobody was looking. They would surely not notice just one missing chicken tonight.

"Well, Joseph. You have had another eventful holiday." Mr Brown said. "I wonder what will happen next holiday. I dread to think." He laughed as he threw his arm round his son's shoulders.

CHAPTER 24

The children had been brought back to earth with a bang. Toby and Professor Profundo had left the day after the party on the padang, to return to England. And now they were getting ready to return to school.

"I miss Toby already" Faradilla said. "He has only just gone."

"I know, but I still miss him."

They learned that the Evil Palm Oil Baron had appealed to the Prime Minister to return the bears to him, but the Prime Minister had dismissed his Appeal.

"What cheek!" Joseph was indignant.

One of the villagers had spotted the Fat Supervisor, a lot skinnier now, sitting at the roadside, begging, when he went to market. Not many people were paying her any attention.

"Serves her right." said Ibrahim.

Ah Kong, they were reliably informed, was working as a road sweeper. And the Evil Palm Oil Baron – well, he had disappeared.

"He'll turn up again somewhere, doing something evil." said Vinod. "He cannot help himself. I believe he does not know how to do anything nice."

"Mmmm, perhaps you are right, Vinod." Xin-Hui was licking an ice-lolly, and it was taking all her concentration to finish it before it melted completely in the heat.

"You've given me an idea, Xin-Hui. Why don't we make great big ice lollies for the bears. It is so hot, and they would love them, I am sure. We can fill some buckets with water, put them in the big chest freezer, and tip them out."

"That is a good idea."

They set to work finding plastic buckets and filling them with water. It did not take the buckets long to freeze and, a couple of hours later, the children were working hard carrying buckets of ice to the bear enclosure, and tipping the ice out for the bears, who loved it. They sat, clutching the ice with their paws, and gnawing it.

Faradilla nudged Xin-Hui.

"Look at Abu and Chio Bu." Sure enough, the two bears looked very close, sharing an ice block, rubbing snouts with each other.

Xin-Hui giggled. "Perhaps we shall have some baby bear cubs, after all." Aishah called them.

"Come along, children. Time to go home. School tomorrow!"

CHARACTERS

Joseph Brown & parents:	Mr & Mrs Brown
Vinod Singh & parents:	Mr & Mrs Singh
Chan Xin- Hui & parents:	Mr & Mrs Chan
Ibrahim Suleiman & parents)	Yusof Suleiman
Faradilla Suleiman)	Aishah Suleiman
Katak	The dog
"The Evil Palm Oil Baron", Lee	Palm Oil plantation owner, who burns down the forest.
Ah Kong	The evil palm oil baron's overseer
The Fat Supervisor	Supervisor of the bile farm
Tunku	Orang Utan family
Puteri	
Number One Son (later to be called Tuhan)	
Number Two Son	
The Head Man	of the Orang-Asli
Rambut Sutera	Member of the Orang-Asli tribe

Matahari	Elephants
Cahaya Bulan	
Ribut	
Halilintar	
Bijaksana	
Hitam Malam	Bears
Hantu	Hitam Malam's cousin
Orkid	A mother of cubs
Hadiah	A mother of cubs
Abu Chio-Bu	
Kabus Kelabu	
Kulat	
Berminyak	Snake
Professor Profundo	Famous English Botanist.
Toby	his son
Shirley Pooper	second rate reporter
Bert	professional photographer

The Prime Minister (Teo)

GLOSSARY OF TERMS

Anjung	Verandah
Atap	Coconut palm roofing
Bapa	Father
Beja Melayu	For men: longloose shirt, over trousers and short sarong
Betel leaf	From Betel Palm, chewed as digestive aid.
Bijaksana	Wise/tactful
Bomoh	Traditional healer
Cahaya Bulan	Moonlight
Cheong-sam	Traditional kind of fitted Chinese dress
Cicada	Big insect with membranous wings. Males produce high-pitched drone.
Granthi	Sikh, custodian of the Adi Granth
Gurdwara	Sikh temple
Guru	Hindu, spiritual teacher
Halilintar	Thunderbolt

Hitam Malam	Black night
Imam	Islam leader
Kabaya	Blouse worn by Asian women
Kampong	Village
Katak	Frog
Kway Teow	Noodle dish
Liana	Woody climbing plants
Matahari	Sun
Mee Goreng	Fried noodle dish
Murtabak	fried omelette, curried
Nasi Goreng	Mixed fried rice dish
Nepenthes Rajah	A species of pitcher plant
Orang Asli	Native people
Padang	Field
Pak-choi	Green vegetable
Pharmacognocist	One who researches and creates medicines
	From natural sources (plants)
Puteri	Princess
Rafflesia	Plant of Asian forest with giant flower
Rambutan	a fruit
Rendang	Spicy beef dish
Ribut	Storm
Roti	Bread
Roti Prata	Asian omelette
Sambal Prawns	Prawns in sambal sauce
Satay	Skewers of meat served with peanut sauce
Tuhan	Lord
Tunku	Prince